Praise for
The Wolverine and the Flame

"Skillfully crafted, brilliantly detailed, this story, by a fantastic storyteller, moves the reader in every way with mages, red and black dragons, talisman and characters that soar on every page. She even blends in the love of dragonkind making this a recommended read."

~ *Linda L., Fallen Angel Reviews*

"...well written, beautifully paced and had awesome love scenes. I am so glad that talented authors such as Ms. Goings choose to share their stories with those who have none."

~ *Robin Smith, My Book Cravings*

"The Wolverine and the Flame is the third book in the Legends of Mynos series by Rebecca Goings. I think this is the most moving of all the stories in the series. I absolutely loved it! ...The love scenes between Meghan and Ethan are tender and poignant. This is a fantastic story I highly recommend!"

~ *Tara Renee, Two Lips Reviews*

"Again, Rebecca Goings brings her readers back to the magical world of Lyndaria and its characters and dragons. In this story, the action and suspense runs high. ...a great plot, multi-dimensional characters, good dialogue and a world that is rich in characters and action. No true blue lover of fantasy should miss this great series. ...it rates up there amongst the greats of high fantasy authors."

~ *Valerie, Love Romances and More*

Look for these titles by
Rebecca Goings

Now Available:

The Cursed Hearts Series:
Hearts Eternal (Book 1)
Hearts Unbound (Book 2)

The Legends of Mynos Series:
The Wolverine and the Rose (Book 1)
The Wolverine and the Jewel (Book 2)

The Leather and Lace Series:
High Noon

The Wolverine and the Flame

Rebecca Goings

A SAMhAIN PUBLISHING, LTD. publication.

Samhain Publishing, Ltd.
577 Mulberry Street, Suite 1520
Macon, GA 31201
www.samhainpublishing.com

The Wolverine and the Flame
Copyright © 2008 by Rebecca Goings
Print ISBN: 978-1-59998-812-2
Digital ISBN: 1-59998-544-6

Editing by Imogen Howson
Cover by Dawn Seewer

First Samhain Publishing, Ltd. electronic publication: August 2007
First Samhain Publishing, Ltd. print publication: June 2008

Dedication

To Terry Brooks, David Eddings and especially, C.S. Lewis, for inspiring within me a love of fantasy ever since I was a little girl. Without you, the entire series The Legends of Mynos would never have been written.

Chapter One

Meghan smiled and hummed to herself as she tossed her mass of red-gold curls over her shoulder. The day was warm with a slight breeze that tugged at her loose tendrils, making her nestle them behind her ear. It was going to be a good day, she could feel it. The clouds were white and puffy as they meandered across the sky and birds sang their happy tunes, flitting from tree to tree.

The fact that she was doing laundry did nothing to hinder her good mood as she reached into the basket to pull out another wet skirt. On a day like today, it was almost an offense to stay inside.

While she bent over to grab another article of clothing, her hair once again spilled over her shoulder. With a sigh, Meghan tossed it back and thought of her twin brother Duncan. Growing up, he'd been the ultimate tease, pulling hard on her fiery locks any chance he could get, even making her cry on more than one occasion. Now they were both grown, he only did it as a soft, loving gesture. Ever since their parents died on that horrible day so long ago, Sir Duncan of Marynville, a king's knight in the Order of the Wolverine, had stopped at nothing to provide for his sister.

A sudden sadness threatened to end her jovial mood as she thought of her parents, cut down by the army of Dark Knights who had decimated the village of Marynville three years before. She'd escaped her own torturous death by hiding in a pile of leaves behind the cottage. Never in her life had she been so scared, knowing that at any moment they might find her. She shuddered to think what the Dark Knights might have done to her if they had.

But the dragon Mynos had been victorious that day. She could even remember watching from the embers of the village as the dragon flew low in the sky, spewing his magical fire on the army threatening Castle Templestone. She'd heard wonderful stories of Mynos from her brother but refused to come with him to the castle in order to meet the dragon. He just seemed too...intimidating.

Now that it was known King Brennan, Queen Lily, and their entire family had been slain at the hands of the insane Lord Merric, the ancient dragon had chosen Sir Geoffrey of Emberdale as the new king of Lyndaria. Meghan had heard plenty of stories of him as well, even meeting him once as he rode through town with Duncan a little more than a year ago while he was still just another Wolverine.

She envied King Geoffrey's relationship with his wife, Queen Arianna. Theirs was a love she longed for herself, wishing and hoping she'd find someone to fill the void in her heart.

Rumors flourished about the love of the new king and queen, of how they could hear each other's thoughts and how deeply they felt for each other. It was no secret they had killed the evil dragon Iruindyll years ago, the one who had disguised herself as the dark Queen Darragh. In protecting the kingdom, it was whispered that King Geoffrey had paid the ultimate price on the battlefield.

With his life.

Many believed Queen Arianna had brought him back from the dead, but no one dared ask her. If she were indeed a mage so powerful as to bring a soul back from beyond, there wasn't a single person in the kingdom willing to upset her by asking.

Marynville had been rebuilt not long after victory was claimed over the evil black dragon. Thankfully Meghan's home had only suffered minor fire damage, and the people of the village helped her and Duncan to bury their parents. Now, their graves near the cottage were covered in sweet-smelling wildflowers.

As Meghan reached in her basket for the last tunic to hang, she noticed three men riding solemnly up the road toward her. She recognized them as Wolverines, yet none of them was Duncan.

His red hair, so like hers, would have betrayed him leagues away.

Stepping out from behind her laundry line, Meghan shielded her eyes from the sun and watched them approach. After a few moments, she recognized the man in front as Sir Sebastian himself, Captain of the Guard at Castle Templestone. The two men riding on either side of him, however, she couldn't remember ever meeting. They were both handsome, one of them having long, sandy-colored hair tied back at the nape of his neck while the other's hair was short and almost the color of wheat.

The man with the longer hair seemed saddened by something, his brows knit together as he returned her gaze. In that moment, Meghan wished he would smile. He was so very handsome, and she was sure if he just smiled, he could outshine the sun.

It didn't take long for the three Wolverines to rein their horses to a stop right in front of her, Sebastian tilting his head to her in silent greeting.

"Sir Sebastian." She smiled. "To what do I owe this visit? And where is Duncan?"

The men glanced at each other before Sebastian spoke. "Meghan, this is Sir Ethan of Krey and Sir Joshua of Korenth."

"How do you do?" she said politely, making eye contact with both of them. The man she had been pondering, Sir Ethan, gazed back at her with hollow eyes.

Without a word, he dismounted and handed his reins to Sebastian. Standing before her, he took her hand and kissed it softly. A shiver raced through Meghan's body.

"Is something the matter, milord?" she whispered to him, taking in his despondent demeanor.

"My lady Meghan," he began, "I'm afraid we come with bad tidings."

"And what might that be on such a fine day, Sir Ethan?"

His dark brown eyes roved her face and he blinked a few times, inhaling deeply. Turning back to his horse, he reached for a sheathed weapon tucked under his saddle. Taking it almost reverently in both hands, Ethan once again faced her and knelt in the dirt.

"I made a promise to Sir Duncan of Marynville, that if anything should happen to him, I would protect you in his stead. I know you have not met me before this day, but please understand that I made a vow to your brother and I intend to uphold it."

"What are you talking about?" she asked, glancing nervously at the other two Wolverines. They watched with silent sadness. A sudden fear crept into her heart, chilling her to the bone. "What has happened?"

"Milady," Ethan began as he pulled the polished weapon

out of its sheath, "Sir Duncan was killed by Lord Merric of Westchester shortly after Merric murdered the royal family."

Meghan froze. The world fell away from her feet. "What did you just say?" she whispered as hot tears pooled in her eyes.

"Your brother is gone," Ethan told her gently, taking her hand once more. "If I could meet you under any other circumstances, please know I wish it were so. But I come to you as the bearer of his blade, a blade that has been passed down through your family, as is tradition among the Wolverines. And so, sweet lady, I present to you Swiftgleam, your brother's sword."

Meghan covered her mouth to silence her sobs, her vision swimming. "Oh my God! He's gone? *Duncan's gone?*"

Unable to accept the weapon in Sir Ethan's hand, Meghan simply crumpled to the ground, weeping and moaning. Her brother was dead. How could that be possible? How could he be dead? Meghan wanted to crawl out of her own skin, only just realizing she was screaming.

From out of nowhere, strong arms encircled her and she leaned into them. "Not Duncan! No... He can't be dead. *He can't be!*"

Someone breathed soothing words into her ear as fingers stroked her hair, but she barely felt it. Her hands clawed at the one who held her, trying to get as close as possible. She suddenly felt as if she were falling off a cliff, and the sturdy arms holding her were the only things keeping her from sliding into a bottomless void.

Meghan struggled to breathe as her body shook, unable to prevent herself from sobbing. She clutched even harder to the one holding her, knowing that once she let go of him, she would be nothing more than a cold, empty shell.

Somewhere in the back of her mind, she felt those strong

arms pick her up and begin walking with her. She had no idea where he was taking her, nor did she care. Her brother was dead. As far as she was concerned, so was she.

CB

Sir Ethan of Krey felt his eyes mist as he held the sister of his closest friend. He'd spoken to her true, he had indeed promised Duncan he'd look after Meghan if something bad should happen to him. Ethan had thought his friend was simply being paranoid, perhaps having had a dream the night before that might have led him to believe his demise was imminent. Ethan had simply wanted to placate him, telling him he would look after Meghan to ease his mind.

But Duncan's premonition proved right after all, as Lord Merric had released his anger on the poor man. The incensed lord had flung him with such magical force that almost every bone in his body had been crushed as he slammed against the stone wall of the corridor beyond the throne room at Castle Templestone. Duncan never had a chance.

Now here Ethan sat, in the dirt outside Duncan's family cottage in Marynville, holding his beautiful twin sister as her body shuddered from the news of his death.

It wasn't in Ethan's nature to hurt a woman, and the guilt he now felt was almost unbearable. He knew he hadn't been the one to kill Duncan, but hearing Meghan's pitiful cries as she clutched him sliced through his heart regardless.

"You'll be all right. I promise you. I promise. I will take care of you." His words were swallowed by Meghan's wails, and he had no idea if she heard him or not. Trying desperately to calm her, he stroked her hair and pulled her closer, taking in her sweet scent and cursing himself for breaking her heart.

"Ethan." Sebastian's voice drifted from behind him. "Why don't you take her inside? There is a crowd growing out here."

Looking around, he could see a few villagers who'd stopped what they were doing to watch the scene unfold. Without a word, Ethan scooped Meghan in his arms and carried her inside the small cottage, kicking the door shut behind him.

The one-room cottage was clean and tidy, with a pot simmering above a cook-fire in the fireplace. The heavenly scent of whatever was steaming inside permeated the air. A tiny wooden table with only two chairs was pushed against one of the walls, and on the far side of the room, a bed sat under an open window with the woolen blanket tucked neatly under the pillow. Ethan had to smile at that. The woman lived alone, and yet she still made her bed to perfection.

Striding over to it, he pulled the blanket back and laid her down, amazed at the force with which she clung to him. He'd intended to simply lay her on the bed in order for her to cry into her pillow, but Meghan refused to let go of him, forcing him to kneel at her bedside.

"Don't leave me," she choked out. "I...I don't want to be alone. I can't...be alone."

Closing his eyes, Ethan sighed and rubbed her shoulders. Her words melted him. He'd never been able to abide a woman's tears.

"I'm not leaving you, Meghan," he whispered. At his words, her hold on him loosened, yet she still embraced him, hiding her face in his neck and sniffling as she wept.

After a little while, her sobs quieted and she leaned back to look at him. Her eyes resembled two shining green emeralds ringed with wet lashes. Sniffling once again, she attempted to wipe her face, trying hard to fight back more tears that threatened to fall.

"Are you hungry?" he asked. She shook her head. "Thirsty?"

"No."

Reaching up to her face, Ethan tucked a stray lock of red-gold hair behind her ear. He didn't say another word, but simply regarded her as she glanced away, and leaned her back into her pillow. Once he pulled the blanket over her, Ethan tried hard to ignore the fact that she was no longer seeking solace in his arms. Offering her comfort seemed the only thing he could do for her. He wished he could do more.

"There, now. You get some rest." As he stood, she caught his hand in hers.

"Don't go," she implored again, the fear and dread at the thought of being alone apparent in her eyes.

"Meghan." He looked down at her, squeezing her hand. "I made a promise to your brother. Now I'm making one to you. I will not leave you."

She nodded, bit her lip, and let his hand go, closing her eyes as she took a shuddering breath. Ethan wished he could take all her despair into his own heart. With sagging shoulders, he propped Duncan's sword against the wall and sighed, staring long and hard at the sheathed weapon.

As Meghan cried softly into her pillow, Ethan turned away and ran his fingers through his hair. If he had to move Heaven and Earth to see her smiling again, so be it.

Chapter Two

"How is she?"

Closing the door gently behind him, Ethan sighed, meeting his captain's eye.

"Not good. She's only just drifted off to sleep."

The sun barely hovered above the horizon as evening settled in. Only a few hours had passed, and yet it felt like an eternity. Nothing could have prepared Ethan for the pain that ripped through his own heart at the sight of Meghan's tears.

Sebastian laid his hand on Ethan's shoulder and smiled sadly. "News of death is never taken well, my friend. Will you be all right?"

Rubbing his eyes, he nodded, weariness already sagging his shoulders.

"Take this," Sebastian urged, holding out his hand. Within his palm lay a beautiful green gem, large and round, glittering in the dying rays of the sun. "We'll take your horse back to the castle and you can return with the Emerald of Estriel when you're ready."

"Are you sure, Seb?" Ethan licked his lips in trepidation. He'd never actually used the gem the dragon Mynos had made as a portal stone. Perhaps he wouldn't be able to work its magic.

Sebastian chuckled. "There's nothing to it. Just ask it to take you to a place you've been before, like the bailey of the castle for instance, and it will open a portal for you. But do not try to talk to Mynos through it."

"Why not?" Ethan took the gem and gazed into it, holding it up to the light.

Sebastian smiled and mounted his horse. "That should be obvious, Ethan. Malnan has returned to him again in the flesh. Even though the Emerald can link with the Crystal, I would hate for you to face the wrath of a dragon for disturbing his reunion with his mate."

"Of...of course," Ethan stammered, clearing his throat. "Well then, I guess I'll see you soon."

"Take care of her, Ethan." Sebastian nodded his head toward the cottage. "She has no one else."

With that, he and Sir Joshua turned their horses and walked back up the road, leading Ethan's mount behind them.

Sighing once more, Ethan turned and opened the door, entering the small house. His stomach growled furiously, but he refused to eat the soup over the fire, wanting instead for Meghan to have something hot to eat once she awakened. Looking through her makeshift kitchen, he found a few rolls and spread two pats of her homemade butter on them.

Ethan sat at the tiny table and ate his fare, his gaze wandering over to the woman in a fitful slumber not more than a few feet away. Was this what King Geoffrey had felt when he'd vowed to protect Arianna all those years ago? Her entire family had been killed by the Dark Knights—all except for her and her Uncle Seth, who'd been brainwashed to fight for Queen Darragh's army. Arianna had been whisked away from her farm by Geoffrey, who'd only been a mere Wolverine at the time. He'd vowed to protect her, to look out for her and be her guardian.

18

Perhaps when Ethan returned to the castle, he would seek out the king and ask him what he should do now. His eyes stung as he stole another glance at Meghan, taking in her red, puffy eyes as she slept.

"I'll take care of her, Duncan," he whispered fervently to himself. "I promise you. Even if I have to die myself to do it."

☳

Meghan awoke to the darkened hut with only the red glow of the coals on her hearth for light. She was exhausted, feeling as if a thousand wild horses had trampled her beneath their pounding hooves. Sitting up in bed, she rubbed her eyes and sighed, hearing the soft breathing of the man on the other side of the room.

Looking toward the sound, she saw the shadowed form of the one who'd told her about Duncan's death. His head was cradled in his arms as he leaned on the table top, sleeping. In that position, the point of his sheathed sword rested on the ground, twisting against his hip, and she silently wondered how he was even comfortable.

In the dim light she admired the lines of his face, relaxed in sleep. He'd said his name was Sir Ethan, and he was indeed a handsome man. Meghan wanted to wake him, to ask him so many questions about her brother, how he died and how close they'd actually been as friends. She seemed to remember him telling her of a promise he'd made Duncan, about looking after her if anything should befall him.

Leave it to Duncan to worry about his sister if there wasn't a man present in her life. Plenty of men had offered for her hand, but none of the men in Marynville struck her fancy, or that of her brother's. Duncan had always been protective of her, sometimes overly so, taking his role as the older brother to the extreme despite the fact he'd been only a mere five minutes older than she.

But whoever this Sir Ethan of Krey was, it was obvious to Meghan her brother had trusted him enough to make him promise to watch over her.

Meghan stood, holding her stomach as it growled. Hopefully Sir Ethan had left her enough soup to eat. As soon as she reached the pot, she gasped at the sight. It was still full.

How long had it been since the Wolverines rode through the village? She surmised it must have been early afternoon when they came, and who knew what time it was now? The moon was high and the stars twinkled in the sky, with hardly any lights burning in the nearby cottages. The poor man must be starving.

Sniffling as she found two bowls in her kitchen, she glanced back at him and felt a warmth spread through her heart. Sir Ethan of Krey had just proven himself to be both chivalrous and considerate. The fact that he'd stayed when she asked him to made her bite her lip to keep the sobs from escaping.

She set the full bowls on the table and gently shook his shoulder.

"Sir Ethan?"

He moaned as his body shifted, but he didn't awaken. His long hair tumbled over his eye and Meghan reached up to smooth it away.

"Sir Ethan?" she said again.

Opening his eyes, he suddenly snapped his head up. "Meghan?" He stood without warning, his hand on the hilt of his sword, glancing around the room as if looking for brigands. "Are you all right, milady?"

"I will be," she told him, placing her hand on his arm and feeling his muscles relax underneath her fingertips.

"Please forgive me for falling asleep," he implored. The look in his eyes told her he'd meant to stay awake, guarding her into the night. She smiled gently at him.

"It is late and you have not yet eaten. Will you eat with me?"

"Milady, that soup is for you. I can wait until I return to the castle."

At the thought of him leaving her, a sudden panic settled into her heart. "Please? Please eat with me, Sir Ethan. It is late, and you have not had any food. Duncan used to love my soup. Besides, there is more than enough for both of us."

Nodding, Ethan pulled out a chair for her and sat after she did.

"I must confess to eating a few of your rolls," he told her.

"I am glad. I'd feel guilty if I'd known you were starving while I slept the night away."

"Do not worry about me, milady," he told her. "I've gone without food for longer than this."

As Ethan took a bite of the tender meat, he closed his eyes and seemed to savor the taste.

"Mmm, this is really good," he said.

"Thank you. The carrots and potatoes are from my very own garden."

"Delicious."

Meghan stared into her bowl. Sir Ethan was not only chivalrous, he was quite charming as well, and she blushed under his scrutiny.

"Thank you for giving me Duncan's sword," she whispered after a few minutes of silence.

21

"It is tradition, milady. The swords of the Wolverines are passed down through the families. Perhaps one day your son will wear it with pride."

Meghan nodded as she glanced at it, propped against the wall.

"Will you be leaving for the castle soon?" she asked, trying to keep the disappointment from lacing her voice. She lived alone in the cottage, and yet for the first time in her life, she actually felt *alone*. She silently dreaded when Sir Ethan would take his leave.

"I will depart when you are ready," he told her.

She looked up at him. "Ready?"

"To come with me."

Meghan's heart suddenly slammed to life. Come with Ethan? To the castle?

"You want me to go with you?"

He nodded. "I'm assuming you'll want to pay your respects to your brother's grave. And I'm sure King Geoffrey himself will want to give you his condolences. Sir Duncan was a good friend of his as well."

Meghan's belly roiled inside of her and she had to push her soup away. Covering her face with her hands, she sighed and felt Ethan's warm hand on her shoulder.

"I am sorry for upsetting you."

"I loved him," she choked out.

"I know."

"I loved him so much!" Once again, she felt her tears break free as the sobs ripped out of her. She didn't know how he'd done it, but upon opening her eyes, she realized she was sitting on Ethan's lap. He held her to him gently, as if he didn't want to break her while he rocked back and forth. Clutching onto his shoulders, she cried into his neck.

Even though this man had been a mere stranger to her just that morning, she felt a bond with him through her grief, and knew he was hurting as much as she was. Duncan was gone and there was nothing she could do to change that. But as she held on to Ethan, she felt as if he anchored her from the storm of her own emotions.

"Thank you, Sir Ethan," she suddenly said, her voice wavering.

"For what?" he asked, stroking her hair.

"For staying with me. Thank you for staying."

As she sat with her head tucked under his chin, she felt his arms tighten around her.

"You are most welcome, milady," he whispered in her ear.

Chapter Three

"It's called the Emerald of Estriel."

Meghan gasped as Ethan held up the green gem between them. They had both stood from the chair only a few moments before, feeling somewhat awkward about their sudden intimacy. Ethan pulled out the portal stone, explaining to her how it worked.

"Mynos made this?" she asked, her eyes round.

Ethan nodded. "Lord Merric killed a lot more than your brother and the royal family. He also slew Malnan, Mynos's mate. Mynos then consecrated her body with his magics, and this gem was born. He named it after his sister and enchanted it as a portal stone."

"And it will take you anywhere?"

"Within reason. It will only take you to places you've been before. Do you want to hold it?"

Meghan looked at him in fright. "Oh I don't think so, Sir Ethan."

"It won't hurt you. This is what will take us to the castle."

Licking her lips, she glanced back at the gem sitting snugly in the palm of his hand. She touched its cool surface. Feeling bolder, she lifted it out of Ethan's hand. It wasn't very heavy, but it sparkled even though there wasn't much light in the cottage.

Meghan clutched it with both hands for fear of dropping it. She shook with excitement as she examined the jewel, not believing she was actually holding a talisman made by Mynos himself.

"You...you said that this was made from the consecrated body of Malnan?"

"Yes," Ethan answered.

"But I have heard rumors, whisperings that Malnan has returned in the flesh."

"Yes, it is true," he said as he nodded.

"How is that possible?"

"There is another gem, somewhat like this, but lavender in color and in the shape of a teardrop. It is known as Malnan's Jewel. It is not enchanted like the Emerald or the Crystal, rather, it is a vessel for the soul of Malnan. She bonded herself to it moments before she died millennia ago during the battle in which all of dragonkind fell. It wasn't until recently that the gem was found and Malnan was able to come back to life through an unblemished dragon's egg found in the King's Mountains."

"But Lord Merric killed her again?"

"Yes. Imagine the grief Mynos must have felt at losing his mate twice."

"How horrible!"

"Indeed it was. But Malnan's soul was once again pulled into her gem as it had been eons ago. As soon as Merric was defeated, Sebastian and his wife, the Lady Jewel, were able to bring Malnan's Jewel back to the cave where another dragon's egg was found. Malnan has returned yet again to Mynos."

"They must truly love each other." Meghan was unable to hide the awe in her voice.

"The story of Mynos and Malnan is indeed a tragic one. But they are finally together now, after all they have endured."

Meghan couldn't help but sniffle at Ethan's story. Being reminded of the love between the dragons made her yearn for a love just as strong for herself.

"Are you all right?"

"Yes, Sir Ethan," she answered with a watery smile. "It was just such a touching story."

After a few moments of silence, Ethan smoothed his hair and sighed, retrieving the Emerald from her hand. "Why don't you get some more sleep? We'll go back to Castle Templestone in the morning."

"No, please. I'm tired, but I don't think I can sleep any longer."

"All right. Would you like to go now?"

"How long will I be there?"

"As long as you like, milady."

"I...I..."

"What?" Ethan asked, concerned.

"I don't have anything to wear that would be fitting for King Geoffrey's court."

Ethan smiled at that, making Meghan's stomach turn inside her. It was the first time she'd seen him smile, and she remembered thinking just that afternoon that if he smiled he could outshine the sun.

She hadn't even been close.

Sir Ethan was a breathtaking man, and she found herself staring at him, suddenly forgetting for a moment what they were talking about.

"Do not worry about your clothes, milady. The king has no use for...foofery."

Ethan's smile was contagious. She couldn't help a small chuckle that escaped her. "*Foofery*, Sir Ethan?"

His smile widened, revealing his straight teeth to her. "Yes indeed, Lady Meghan. Foofery can be prized much too highly by those who do not know better."

"All of my clothing is still hanging on the laundry line."

"Do not worry about those clothes." Ethan gave her a grand flourish of his arm. "You will look much better without them."

Meghan shot him a look of surprise at his words before she saw color steal into his cheeks.

"What I meant to say, milady, is that you will surely be given gowns to wear, not that you'd be...that you'd... Well," he said, clearing his throat nervously, "you understand."

Meghan tried hard not to laugh at him. He was obviously flustered at what he'd just said.

"Well then, it seems the only thing I'll need is this." She drifted to the far wall of the cottage. Bending down, she grabbed her brother's sword and held it to her chest with both hands.

"All right. I'm ready."

☙

Meghan felt as if she'd been doused with a bucket of icy water as she stepped through the portal made by the Emerald of Estriel. However, the chill vanished once she was completely through the magical doorway. Sir Ethan stepped through a moment after she did, and the portal closed silently behind them.

They stood in Ethan's chambers, a darkened room with a cold hearth and a large, unmade bed. The curtains above a window were pulled back and a few chairs clustered in front of the fireplace.

He'd suggested they travel to his room, as walking through a magical portal in the courtyard of the castle would cause too much of a fuss. It was late at night, and the men patrolling the walls didn't need to be spooked. Neither did Meghan need the extra stress a call to arms would bring.

Still clutching on to her brother's sword, she didn't know what to do. Ethan seemed embarrassed about the state of disarray of his chambers, and ushered her to a chair before attempting to make his bed. When he finished, he bent to light a fire in the hearth.

"Please excuse the mess, milady," he said. "I wasn't expecting a visitor."

Meghan gave him a small smile. "Do not fret, Sir Ethan. I am not offended."

"It is still a while before dawn. When the maids are roused, I will order a room to be prepared for you."

"Thank you. I would like that."

"Are you sure you do not want to sleep? My bed is very comfortable." Once he said that, he coughed awkwardly behind his hand while a deep red blush crept up his cheeks.

"I'm sure your bed is quite soft, milord," she said with a grin. "But I am perfectly happy right where I am. Perhaps I'll just sit in front of the fire for awhile."

Ethan nodded and looked away, smoothing a few hairs that had slipped from the leather strap at the nape of his neck.

"Would you like to play a game?"

Meghan glanced at him with an arched brow. "A game?"

Nodding, Ethan smiled at her. "Sure. I'll teach you. It's easy and quite enjoyable. In fact, I won many of Duncan's hard-earned silver ladies playing with him."

"Ah, so you're a gambler?"

"No, milady, I'm a swindler, and I'm not ashamed to admit it." His eyes sparkled, making Meghan chuckle in spite of herself.

"I'm afraid I have no coins with which to make it worth your while."

"Do not worry yourself about that." He patted the fur rug next to him as he sat in front of the fire. "I'll simply teach you without betting. How's that?"

Reaching above him onto a small table, Ethan pulled down two odd-shaped dice.

"All right."

"Just a moment, milady," he said as he unbuckled his sword belt. "Sitting like this with Firefury strapped to my waist is most uncomfortable."

Meghan glanced down at the sheathed weapon as he leaned it against the wall.

"Is that the name of your sword?"

"Indeed," he answered, gesturing her to give him Swiftgleam as well. When both swords were propped against the wall, he turned back to her. "These two swords have seen many a sparring match together."

"Oh?"

Ethan nodded with a smile. "Duncan and I used to practice our swordplay with each other. I fear my sword will miss his."

"They are together now," Meghan said, peeking at him through her lashes. Ethan sat and regarded her for a few moments before nodding once again.

"That they are, milady."

"So how do you play?" Meghan wanted to know.

"This game is called 'Dragon's Tooth'. It is named that because these dice resemble the teeth of a dragon." Ethan held one to show her. Flat on one end and pointed on the other, there were four sides to it, resembling a pyramid. On each point was a picture. Upon examining the die, Meghan could see the figure of a man, a dragon breathing flame, a glowing sword, and a crown.

"Now, you have one die, and I have the other," Ethan explained. "Each one of these pictures corresponds with each other. With each roll of our dice, there is always a winner, and a loser, and sometimes there can be a draw. The dragon eats the man, the man claims the crown, the crown takes the sword, and the sword slays the dragon. Each picture has a strength and a weakness. So roll yours and let's see what you get."

Meghan rolled her die on the floor. The picture of the man turned up.

"All right, let's see what I get."

Ethan rolled, and the dragon breathing fire spun face up.

"This dragon here wins the match, as he burns the helpless villager to a crisp."

"Oh!" Meghan gasped as Ethan chuckled. "How horrid!"

"Roll again, milady."

Meghan did, and this time she rolled the crown.

"Good one. Now I'll go."

Ethan's die rested on the man. "Ooo, the man claims the crown. I win again."

Rolling once more, Meghan got the dragon. She smiled at Ethan as he picked up his die. He rolled a crown.

"Ah, a draw."

Once again, Meghan rolled the dragon. Ethan's die rested on the sword. "The sword slays the dragon. Not your day, milady," he said with a wide grin.

"I can believe you are a swindler, Sir Ethan."

"Indeed, Lady Meghan," he told her, trying to hold back his chuckles. "We are playing with my enchanted dice!"

"Oh, you scoundrel!" Meghan squealed as she tossed her die back at him. She couldn't help but giggle as he flinched from the flying projectile. It hit his shoulder and bounced harmlessly off.

"Never fear, milady, I have another set!"

"You think I'm going to play again with you?" Meghan placed her hands on her hips in mock anger.

"I promise to be good. No cheating."

"I have your word?"

"On my honor as a knight in the Order of the Wolverine, milady. Besides, we have Firefury and Swiftgleam as witnesses. If either of them observe me cheating, I give them full reign to announce my detestable practices to my fellow knights."

"They can do that?" Meghan looked at him with her eyes wide.

"The swords of the Wolverines are enchanted, milady. Indeed they can talk with one another."

Glancing at the swords, Meghan licked her lips. "All right, Sir Ethan. I'll take you up on it. I hope you don't mind being beaten by a woman."

Ethan's hearty laughter filled his chamber. Meghan's skin prickled at the sound of it. Her body suddenly warmed and it had nothing to do with the fire in the hearth.

Chapter Four

Ethan watched Meghan as she slept soundly on his fur rug a few hours later. The sky pinkened with the dawn and he knew he should get some sleep as well, yet he couldn't help but watch her as she softly breathed in slumber.

He'd taken the blanket from his bed and laid it over her, smiling to himself when she mewled in her sleep. They'd played Dragon's Tooth for awhile and indeed he'd been bested by her a few times. Her eyes were still shadowed from the news of Duncan's passing, yet the few hours they'd spent together seemed to lighten her spirits.

Meghan had yawned, making Ethan suggest she lie back as they played. But it hadn't been long before her eyes closed and her breathing evened. He wasn't about to wake her. She needed all the rest she could get.

Her red-gold hair, that had been so odd and out of place on her brother Duncan, seemed perfect on her, spread upon the rug like gossamer flames. Ethan studied her hair for a long while. The dying firelight played across the strands, bringing out her highlights of gold, and Ethan had to turn away or risk running his fingers through it.

Her eyes had captivated him as well—a deep shade of green he hadn't seen on any other woman. They reminded him of the Lady Jewel's eyes. Even though Sebastian's wife had eyes the same lavender color as Malnan's Jewel, both she and Meghan could claim their eyes were unique among women.

Ethan smiled as he thought of Lady Jewel, remembering all the times he'd tried to win her away from Sebastian. He had fought a losing battle and he knew it. Anyone could tell Jewel's heart belonged only to the Captain of the Guard. But that hadn't stopped Ethan from trying.

Since then, barely a handful of women had caught his eye, most of them traveling to the castle with their families to swear fealty to King Geoffrey before leaving with their entourage a few days later. He'd never actively pursued any of them. What would be the point?

Ethan was tired getting what he could where he could. He wanted stability, a wife, and the prospect of a family as Sebastian or even King Geoffrey had. The problem was finding a good woman.

Meghan stirred and rolled over, tucking the blanket under her chin as she moved. Ethan had to smile. She was indeed a beautiful woman, but she was more than that. What little time he'd spent with her proved she was a woman he wanted to get to know better. And the knowledge she was his to protect filled him with pride.

He'd never been needed by a woman before, and he enjoyed it. Lying on the rug next to her, he placed his hands under his head and stared at the ceiling. Duncan had asked him to take care of his sister, and at the time, Ethan had balked at the request. Now, as he chanced another glance at the woman sleeping beside him, he silently wondered if Duncan's sister was the one woman he might be able to settle down with.

Right before he closed his eyes and drifted off, Ethan could hear the faint buzzing of the two enchanted swords, still right where he put them, propped against the wall.

CB

A loud knock woke Meghan. Opening her eyes, she shielded them from the sunlight streaming in through the window and tried to get her bearings. Where was she?

Her eyes were still heavy from sleep as she laid her head back down on the soft fur. Fur?

Something rustled next to her, then a few swift footsteps followed by the sound of an opening door. Was she still in Ethan's room? Meghan tried to look around, but sleep clouded her vision.

Rubbing her eyes, she yawned as words floated over to her.

"Good God, what are *you* doing here?" Ethan sounded shocked.

"I'm here to retrieve my Emerald," a deep voice answered out in the hall. "I trust you slept well?"

"You cannot come in. You'll scare Meghan half to death!"

"Nonsense. I've never met the sister of Sir Duncan. I'm sure she'll be delighted to meet me."

The hinges on the door creaked as Ethan exclaimed, "Mynos, wait. *Mynos!*"

At the sound of that name, Meghan sat up and gasped, sleep suddenly forgotten. A man stood smiling down at her, his skin a golden hue and his hair shining gold in the light of the sun streaming through the window. But his eyes... His eyes were what unnerved her, having slits for pupils, much like a cat. She remembered stories Duncan had told her of the dragon, and those eyes were mentioned time and time again.

He turned his head to smile at Ethan, and Meghan could see the highlights in his golden hair shimmer with every color of the rainbow.

"Lady Meghan, this is the dragon Mynos. Mynos, this is Sir Duncan's sister, Meghan," Ethan said with a sigh.

"How do you do, Daughter?" the dragon asked her.

Meghan simply stared with her mouth wide open. She couldn't do much more than gape at him. This was the same creature she'd seen flying in the sky a few years ago, decimating Queen Darragh's army with his fiery breath alone. How could she not be cowed in front of him?

"Fear not," he told her in a gentle tone. "I will not harm you. You are safe with me. Your brother, Sir Duncan, was a kind and loyal Wolverine. He will be greatly missed here at the castle."

"Th—thank you," she stammered, her entire body shaking. "I will m—miss him too."

Ethan stepped over to her and crouched low, placing a hand on her shoulder. Its warmth seemed to radiate throughout her entire body, calming her nerves.

"Mynos speaks true, milady. He will not harm you."

Tearing her gaze away from the dragon, she glanced at Ethan. His eyes softened when she nodded. He stood as well, offering her his hand. Meghan took it gladly, but did not let go once she was on her feet. Ethan gave her a gentle squeeze.

Mynos wandered to the bedside table where Ethan had deposited the Emerald the night before. The dragon picked it up and turned it in his hand, making it flash in the light. Meghan could see the faint hint of a smile on his face.

"Did you enjoy your journey to the castle, Daughter?" he asked.

"Very much," she told him. "I've never seen a magical portal before. I was cold when I stepped through."

"That's the magical barrier you passed. The Emerald alerted me the moment you two arrived at the castle."

Ethan stiffened. "I—I'm sorry, Mynos," he said, suddenly remembering Sebastian's words from the evening before about not disturbing the dragon.

"Do not worry yourself, Son," Mynos said with a grin. "Malnan was exhausted at the time. I doubt she had strength enough to crack an eye."

Ethan laughed at that, truly happy for the dragon and his mate. "Where is she now?"

"Still resting. I fear she'll be resting for quite awhile to come."

He couldn't help it, Ethan laughed even harder at the sly look on Mynos's face. "You're a dragon after my own heart, did you know that, Mynos?" He wiped tears of mirth from his eyes.

Meghan blushed and turned away, apparently too embarrassed by the intimate topic of conversation.

"It seems as if we've embarrassed the lady with our plain talk," Mynos said, still grinning.

Ethan smiled down at Meghan, who gave him a shy grin of her own. Her cheeks once again bloomed with color, and he instantly noticed the hint of a dimple in her right cheek. It was all he could do not to stare at it.

"I've taken it upon myself to have chambers made up for you, Meghan," Mynos said. "Your room is just down the hall, close to Sir Ethan's chambers, as I know he is your sworn protector now."

"Again, I thank you, Mynos," she exclaimed, looking back and forth between Ethan and the dragon.

"You should also find a steaming tub and a bureau full of dresses, devoid of any foofery."

It was Ethan's turn to gawk at the dragon. "Were you eavesdropping on us last night, Mynos?"

"Eavesdropping? No. Overhearing? Yes. When the bearer of the Emerald feels a strong emotion, I can feel it too through the Emerald's bond with the Crystal. And your emotions last night, Sir Ethan, were the strongest I've felt yet."

A hot blush crept up Ethan's cheeks at that moment. Meghan turned to him, as if not understanding the dragon's words. But as Mynos smiled with his golden eyes shining, Ethan knew without a doubt the dragon was aware of his fond ponderings toward Duncan's sister.

"Come, Daughter," Mynos said, sparing Ethan any more discomfort. "Let me show you to your room."

Chapter Five

King Geoffrey should have been working. Piles of paperwork sat on his desk, awaiting his signature. Treaties, writs, and mundane reports from around the castle and the kingdom stared back at him as he sat behind the enormous mahogany desk in his study. Thomas, his overworked steward, had been adamant that the documents must be signed today for the good of the country. But Geoffrey was confident that the kingdom wouldn't collapse if he failed to sign them at this very moment.

Yet ignoring them would only bring twice as much work on the morrow, as the piles seemed never-ending. With a sigh, Geoffrey pushed away from his desk and walked to the large, paned window behind him that stretched almost from floor to ceiling. It looked out over the waves of the Silver Sea, crashing on the rocky beach far below.

Castle Templestone itself sat on the high cliffs of Lyndaria, looking out upon the ocean on one side, and a vast, open field on the other. The city of Marynville was located not too far away, hidden from the castle by a gentle slope in the countryside. The day was beautiful, with the sun shining warm and bright in the sky as white, puffy clouds slowly rolled by.

Geoffrey ran his palm longingly over the hilt of his sword, remembering his days as a Wolverine not so long ago. Quicksilver now rested on his hip where Flameblade had once been, even though he hardly wielded it any longer. He'd become a Wolverine with Flameblade, his father's sword, yet his wife had given him Quicksilver, the weapon of *her* father. It had slain the dragon Iruindyll years ago and had been the very sword used by Mynos at Geoffrey's coronation. But those were not the reasons why he wore it now.

Geoffrey wore Quicksilver on his hip simply because of the way his wife looked at him whenever he did. Arianna's loving gaze made him feel as if he could conquer the world if she but asked. He loved his wife dearly, more than she knew, and that was the only reason Quicksilver was more precious to him than any other blade at the castle.

The dragon was fond of telling him King Benjamin used to wear *his* sword ages ago, having been chosen by the dragon as Ruler of the Four Realms after the death of King Timothy. Geoffrey couldn't imagine the day when he would ever take off his sword. It was a part of him, a part of who he was, and if the castle were ever attacked, he'd be on the battlements, fighting with the rest of his men.

A sharp knock on the doors of his study brought Geoffrey out of his pensive mood. Thankful for another distraction from the hated pile of work on his desk, he turned from the window and smiled.

"Enter."

Sir Ethan of Krey opened the door and closed it behind him, bowing slightly.

"I trust I'm not intruding, Your Majesty?"

Geoffrey's smile widened. "Indeed you are, Ethan, however, yours is a most welcome intrusion."

The poor man looked undecided in what he should do, walk out and leave the king in peace, or stay and chat with him as he'd intended.

"Would you like me to leave, Your Majesty?" he asked.

"What I'd like you to do is have a seat and refrain from this 'Your Majesty' nonsense. I've known you for years, Ethan. Call me Geoffrey."

Coughing behind his hand, Ethan nodded his head and sat in one of the overstuffed chairs sitting in front of the king's desk. Geoffrey walked around it and sat on top of the desk itself, pushing piles of paper out of his way to make room.

"To what do I owe this most welcome interruption?"

"Well, Your M—" Ethan began. He cleared his throat. "I mean Geoffrey. I've brought Duncan's sister to the castle and I thought I could talk to you about what I should do, now that she is my responsibility."

"What you should do?"

"Yes. It occurred to me that you and Queen Arianna were once in a similar situation, being her protector and what not. I figured you might know more than I how to handle a situation such as this."

"Ah," Geoffrey said, nodding his head and pursing his lips. "Yes, well, I handled things poorly with my wife before we were wed. I might not be able to tell you what to do, but I can offer you advice on what *not* to do."

Ethan smiled. "I'd like that."

"How do you feel towards her?"

"Well, I'm saddened at her loss. I don't want to see her cry. She's a beautiful girl who deserves happiness in her life."

Geoffrey stared at him for a few uncomfortable moments.

"All right, I admit, I've thought tenderly about her. But she's so vulnerable right now. I'm not sure if what I'm feeling is true affection or merely my desire to protect her."

"How does she feel about you?"

"She likes me well enough, I suppose. I taught her how to play Dragon's Tooth..."

"Oh, tell me you didn't!" He was aghast.

"We played with my legitimate dice, I assure you."

Geoffrey chuckled at that. "So she's making an honest man of you?"

"Hardly, Sire." Ethan grinned.

"Just don't swindle the poor girl."

"Oh no, Geoffrey, I wouldn't even think of it."

"I'm glad to hear that." Jumping off the desk, Geoffrey then paced back and forth in front of Ethan. "You've sworn an oath to Sir Duncan, and I can only assume to her as well, to be her protector, am I correct?"

"Yes," Ethan said with a nod.

"Then my advice to you is this. Do not stifle her. She is a grown woman, used to having freedom and being able to go wherever she chooses whenever she chooses. Try not to worry about her every minute of the day. She lived many long years before you came into her life, I'm sure the lady knows how to take care of her basic needs.

"However," Geoffrey continued, stopping to look Ethan in the eye. "If she yearns for your company, if she requests to sit next to you every night at supper, if she draws close to you and smiles often, do not turn her away. If you feel anything for her, do not *ever* shut her out. I almost lost Arianna because I thought I was doing the right thing by turning my back on her. I thought the best thing for her was to stay far away from me. But I couldn't have been more wrong. She needed me—I was just too blind to see it.

"Arianna has since forgiven me for it, but it has taken me longer to forgive myself, knowing that I caused her pain for no good reason. If you find Meghan has somehow clambered into your heart, then tell her so. It's what Sebastian did. And he's most content with his marriage to Lady Jewel."

"Thank you, Geoffrey, I'll keep that in mind."

"And Ethan?"

"Yes?"

"It is possible that you may have feelings for her that she does not return. If that is the case, you must learn to let her go to find her own husband. Once she does, your role as her protector will be over. It may just be one of the hardest things you'll ever have to do. A sword ripping through your heart is nothing compared to what a woman can do to it."

Taking a deep breath, Ethan nodded and stood. "Thank you."

"Oh, and one more thing," Geoffrey said. Ethan looked at him questioningly. "My wife wishes you the best."

He winked and gave Ethan a secret smile. Turning back to his desk, Geoffrey straightened the papers once again.

Ethan stared at him for a moment. "Be sure to thank her for me," he said as he strode to the door.

"Already done."

Chapter Six

Meghan soaked in the bath for what seemed like hours as the hot water eased away the ache in her muscles. Even after sleeping for a time on Ethan's fur rug, she was still exhausted. She even dozed off in the warm water. But she finally stepped out and donned one of the dresses hanging in the bureau.

Mynos was right, these dresses were devoid of foofery, as Ethan had said. There were many shades of fabric, each decorated with a conservative amount of lace and embroidery. Meghan decided on a light-green dress, the color of mint, with just a hint of lace adorning the neckline and cuffs. It made her own green eyes even brighter and her red hair seemed to smolder against it.

She wove her long tresses into a manageable braid and sighed as she gazed at her reflection in the mirror. Dark circles were beneath her eyes, but there was no hope for it. Every thought of Duncan had her eyes once again stinging with tears. It was all she could do to hold them at bay.

After Mynos had shown her to her room, Ethan had mentioned coming for her a little later to take her to the cemetery where her brother was buried. She wasn't sure if she was ready to see Duncan's grave. It would simply make his death more permanent, a realization Meghan wasn't sure she was prepared for.

Yet at the same time, she wanted to go, for her own peace of mind and to see for herself that Duncan was never coming back.

She'd settled into the window seat of her chambers, looking out upon the ocean with her brooding thoughts, when a knock sounded at her door. She rose and drifted through the room to open it, only to find Sir Ethan on the other side.

His mouth dropped open as he stared at her, taking her in from head to toe. He was silent for so many long moments that Meghan began to blush under his scrutiny.

"Is something the matter, milord?" she asked him, looking down at her dress as if it might be stained.

Ethan coughed behind his hand and shook his head. "Uh, no, milady, not at all," he told her. "It's just that you are very uh...very beautiful in that dress."

"Oh," was all she could think to say as her skin flamed with heat. "Well, th-thank you."

Glancing at him, she noticed he'd taken the time to freshen up as well. His hair was still a little damp and it was pulled back at the nape of his neck. Meghan wondered if he ever wore it down. Many times she'd admired Ethan, yet she knew his hair would only enhance his looks if he wore it down. She supposed his duties around the castle prevented him from wearing it that way. But it wasn't too long, as it barely hung below his shoulders.

"Are you ready?" he asked, bringing her thoughts back to the matter at hand.

Not trusting her voice, she simply nodded and closed her chamber door behind her.

"King Geoffrey has allowed you to pick any flowers you'd like from the royal gardens to lay on Duncan's grave if you wish."

44

"Yes, I would like that."

Ethan turned and led her down the hallway toward the grand staircase.

"Are you feeling better, milady?"

"Somewhat. I am still unimaginably tired."

He nodded. "I can imagine. Duncan's passing still saddens me. He was my closest friend."

"Truly?" Meghan asked, stopping in the middle of the hall. Ethan turned to her.

"Truly. I may have taken advantage of him a time or two...or three," he said with a chuckle, "but Sir Duncan was a good man. I can only hope to be half the man he was."

Meghan took a step closer to him and smiled gently. "You are more like him than you know, Sir Ethan," she whispered. "I appreciate all you have done for me. I don't know where I'd be at this moment without you."

Silence stretched between them as Ethan dropped his gaze to his boots. Meghan's heart went out to him. He might not show his feelings, but she knew he was hurting, perhaps as much as she was.

Closing the gap between them, Meghan curled her arms around his neck and hugged him without a word. Almost instantly, his arms wrapped around her, holding her tight.

"Sir Ethan," she said in his ear, "it's all right to mourn him." His arms tightened at her words. Meghan sighed at the feeling. The only other man to hold her like this had been her brother. Now here she was, in the arms of her brother's closest friend, comforting him over their mutual loss.

"I miss him, Meghan," she heard him say as his voice wavered.

"I do too." She couldn't stop the tears as they fell down her face. Stroking his hair, Meghan turned her face into Ethan's neck and wept.

"I'll never let anything bad happen to you. I promise you."

Pulling away from him slightly, Meghan gave him a watery smile. "I know." Caressing one of his cheeks with her hand, she reached up and kissed his other one.

Ethan's eyes were misty as he gazed down at her, seemingly unwilling to let her go. After a few long moments, he released her, only to grab her hand.

"Come, milady," he said as he tucked her fingers into the crook of his arm. "Let's go pick some flowers."

Meghan held onto his arm with her other hand as well, content to follow him wherever he might lead.

ᙄ

"I don't believe it!" Meghan wandered through the blooms until she stood in front of a beautiful bunch of red flowers with six petals each. "King Geoffrey has Heartfire lilies!"

Ethan smiled at the wonder on her face. "The royal gardens have just about any flower you'd imagine." Many different flowers of many different colors bloomed all around them. A pleasant fragrance floated in the air. The large, three-tiered marble fountain in the middle of the gardens gurgled as the water cascaded down each level. Ethan sat on one of the marble benches surrounding the fountain and watched her.

"These Heartfire lilies were our favorite flowers! Mother planted them near our cottage, but they never grew like this or bloomed quite so magnificently."

"Yes, Geoffrey's royal gardener does seem to know what he's doing. Often he and his entourage are out here tending the flowers."

"These will be perfect. How many may I pick?"

"As many as you desire, milady."

"I think about five should be all right, don't you?"

Ethan smiled and nodded.

As soon as the lilies were in her hand, she smelled them and sighed. "These bring back so many memories."

"All good ones, I hope," Ethan told her, standing and offering his arm once more.

"Mostly," she said with a smile.

After they left the gardens, Ethan led her on a stone path that wound behind the castle. The lilies in her hand trembled as she walked, and she licked her lips nervously.

"We don't have to do this," Ethan said, noticing the tenseness in her body.

Meghan glanced up at him and gave him a weak smile. "Yes, we do," she said. "I need to say goodbye to him."

Ethan patted her hand on his arm. "Let me know if you need some time alone."

Shaking her head, she slid her hand down his arm to lace her fingers with his. "Please don't leave, Sir Ethan. You...you give me strength."

Ethan didn't say a word, but squeezed her hand and continued to lead her on.

It didn't take long before they stood in a large cemetery with headstones everywhere. Looking at them, Meghan noticed that each stone was engraved with the insignia of the Wolverine. They were all graves of the king's knights and their families.

"Come. Over here, milady," Ethan said softly, weaving

through the stones.

Once they finally stopped in front of her brother's grave, Meghan gasped. There on the ground lay three wilted Heartfire lilies, looking as if they'd lain there for days.

She glanced at Ethan with questioning eyes. He shrugged as he looked back at her.

"Do you know who put these here?" Meghan asked him.

"I do not," he told her, his brow furrowing in thought. "But I have a good idea."

"Oh?" Meghan bent to place her fresh flowers on the soft dirt. She caressed the engraving on the headstone that read *Sir Duncan of Marynville*. She could already feel more tears brewing behind her eyes as she sniffled.

"The Lady Vanessa of Arlington, or Lady Arlington as she's known here at the castle."

Meghan looked up at Ethan and squinted. "A woman?"

Ethan smiled and knelt beside her. "An older woman at that. The only thing she wanted in this life was Sir Duncan himself, or so it would seem. They had a short, but torrid affair, one he never talked about. However, from what I gather, Lady Arlington was very much in love with him."

"I've never heard of her."

"As I said, Duncan did not speak of it. I'm not sure why. He was very shy around women. I tried to get him to have some fun with the fairer sex, and not only myself, but Sir Sebastian as well. We were determined to get him to open up. But Lady Arlington...she chased him down and wouldn't take no for an answer."

"Goodness!"

"Duncan must have loved her as well, for he always smiled fondly whenever I brought up the subject. But Lady Arlington herself left the castle a few days ago to return to her estates. I remember seeing her walking through the gardens right before she departed. Perhaps it was she who laid your brother's favorite flower on his grave."

Looking back down at the wilted blossoms for long, silent moments, Meghan could no longer hold it in. Deep sobs ripped through her.

"I loved Duncan so much," she whispered.

Ethan's strong arm curled around her shoulder and instantly she leaned on him for support. Kneeling there in the dirt, she embraced him as she tried to calm her breathing.

"Sir Ethan?"

"What, milady?" he whispered to her, stroking her hair.

Meghan sniffled and shuddered as she pulled back just enough to look into his dark eyes. Once she had, she cupped his cheek with her palm.

"I have no one left in this world. No one but you."

Ethan grabbed her hand to hold it there as he turned his head, kissing her palm.

"Meghan," he said as his eyes searched hers, "I will always be here for you."

Closing her eyes, she savored the sound of her name on his lips. Her palm burned where he had kissed her, and she silently wished he would kiss her fully.

Nodding at his words, she bit her lip and gazed at him through watery lashes.

"I'm so scared," she confessed.

"Do not be. I will take care of you."

"Truly?" she asked in a small voice. "You will not leave?"

"I will not leave." As he spoke, he bent his head lower,

tipping her chin up with his fingers.

Meghan's heart beat erratically at his nearness, and it was all she could do to sit still as his thumb stroked her cheek. The world seemed to drop away at that moment, with only her and Ethan, together in each other's arms.

"What is to become of me?"

"You will live as you have before, yet from now on, I will be with you."

A thrill shot through her at the thought of having Ethan with her forever, watching over her. But did he feel something else for her? Something more?

Laying her head back down on his shoulder, she breathed him in and caressed his neck with her fingers. As his arms tightened around her, Meghan closed her eyes and sighed.

For a brief moment, she pondered what life with Ethan would be like if he became more to her than simply her protector. She found that she liked the idea. Perhaps a little too much.

As she hugged him, Meghan knew it would only be a matter of time before she fell completely in love with him. Sir Ethan of Krey was just too perfect. But could she bear it if he didn't feel the same? She tried hard to banish the thought.

Chapter Seven

As they left the cemetery, Meghan sighed and looked up at the bright blue sky. It was a beautiful day. She savored the feeling of the warm sunshine on her face as she walked. Her heart still ached for her brother, but being with Ethan seemed to dull the pain.

A memory had come back to her upon laying the Heartfire lilies at her brother's grave, one of her father and his many stories from their childhood.

"Sir Ethan?"

"Yes, milady?"

"Did Mynos ever make...a red talisman?"

"A red one?" He turned his head to look at her as they walked, his boots crunching on the gravel of the path.

"I've seen the Emerald of Estriel with my own eyes, and you've talked to me about the Crystal. I just wanted to know if there was a red ruby as well."

"I have not heard of one." Ethan stroked his chin in thought. "There is Malnan's Jewel, a lavender-colored gem that has been fitted into a necklace. But I've never heard the dragons talking about a red one."

"Strange," Meghan said, watching the clouds as they meandered along.

"Why do you ask?"

Meghan squinted at him through the sunlight. "I remembered an old rhyme my father used to tell my brother and me as kids. It was a story meant to scare us and keep us well-behaved. I remember hiding under my blankets at night for fear this red jewel would somehow find me. When I saw the Heartfire lilies, I recalled the story, as the color of the flowers used to remind my father of his tale. Whenever my mother's flowers would bloom, he would tell it to us."

"How did it go?"

"Well, it's a rhyme. My mother always chastised my father for telling it, and yet Duncan and I always managed to do our chores afterward."

"Do you remember it?"

"How could I forget?" She chuckled. "Even now it gives me the chills."

"Then tell it to me. I want to hear it."

"All right, Sir Ethan, but if you end up having nightmares, it is not my fault."

Ethan chuckled at that. "I think I'm beyond getting frightened over a child's rhyme."

Meghan smiled at him. "All right. I'll recite it for you."

Thinking for a moment, she took a deep breath and began.

"In the mountains, black as night,
rests a gem no man can tame.
Red as blood and feared by men
is the gruesome Dragon's Flame.

"Deadly fire is its magic,

meant to burn, mangle, maim.
No one can hope to escape
the wrath of Dragon's Flame.

"Many have sought its power
for their own fortune and fame.
Yet one by one did they succumb
to the horror of Dragon's Flame.

"They did not believe the stories,
thinking all was just a game,
but soon they learned the folly
of trusting Dragon's Flame.

"One brave soul then hid it well,
yet history knows not his name.
To take the madness upon himself
and bury Dragon's Flame.

"Now deep within the Dragon's Death,
it rests in silent shame.
Hungrily it waits for you,
the dreaded Dragon's Flame."

Ethan stopped walking to stare at her with his mouth hanging open. "Good God!" he exclaimed. "Your *father* used to tell you this rhyme?"

Meghan nodded. "He was quite fond of this one. Said his

own father told it to him when he was a child."

"It does sound oddly like one of Mynos's gems. But I know the dragon. He would never make an evil talisman such as this."

"Perhaps he didn't make it."

Ethan pondered that for a moment. "I think it's too much of a coincidence that this rhyme describes a red gem not too unlike the Crystal or the Emerald. I think we should tell this to King Geoffrey."

"Are you serious? But it's just a story!"

"Perhaps, Lady Meghan." Ethan furrowed his brow. "Yet even so, I think it's worth telling the king, and maybe even asking Mynos about it."

"Sir Ethan, I don't want to bother the dragon with a silly rhyme meant to scare children."

"It doesn't hurt to ask, milady," he said, his face grave. "Mynos has lived for many, many centuries. If there is a red ruby in existence, he will know."

Meghan shuddered.

Wrapping his arm around her shoulders, Ethan said, "Come, milady, let's go tell the king."

ᙡ

Queen Arianna sat on the bottom steps of the grand staircase in the main hall of the castle, her voluminous blue skirts spread wide before her. She sat uncaring of who might see her in such an unladylike position, her arm linked with the dragon Malnan's arm, grinning like a fool.

"This is the first time Mynos has let you leave his lair," she said to the dragon with a chuckle. "I take it you two have had some catching up to do?"

Malnan nodded her human head with a mischievous smile, her mass of soft green tresses bouncing with the movement. Her skin also had a pale green hue, as well as her eyes, slitted just as Mynos's golden ones were. "A few millennia to be exact," the dragon said. "I do not believe he is yet finished with me."

Arianna grinned widely at that. "I'm so glad to hear it, Malnan. Mynos was heartbroken when you died a second time. I don't believe I've ever seen him happier than the moment you returned once again in the flesh with Sir Sebastian and the Lady Jewel."

"It is good to be alive again, Your Majesty. The feelings are...most pleasurable."

"I cannot imagine being separated for so long," Arianna told her. "Geoffrey and I have had our fair share of hardships, but nothing like what you and Mynos have had to endure."

"That is not altogether true, Daughter. You lost your mate just as Mynos lost me. The difference is you were able to pull his soul back from beyond. Not to mention the pain both of you went through when you lost the child growing within your belly."

Malnan squeezed Arianna's arm gently. Being reminded of Geoffrey's death a few years ago had Arianna shivering in spite of herself. It was true that she had brought him back through the power of the Crystal, but just thinking of what would have become of her if she hadn't been able to made her shudder. He still bore the mark of the Crystal on his chest, a pinkened circle that reminded her of just how close she'd come to losing him that day.

And her daughter... Arianna didn't like to think about the pain she'd felt when she couldn't follow her child through death's domain as she had once followed Geoffrey. The agony tearing through her belly had erased any concentration she had, and the baby had slipped away. For over a week she hadn't eaten, nor had she emerged from her chambers. It had been the power of the Crystal that had prevented her from getting pregnant for three long years, and it was the power of the Crystal that had taken the life of her daughter when she was finally able to become pregnant. No one could have guessed what prolonged use of the Crystal would do to a woman's body. But ever since then, Arianna had vowed never to touch it again.

The king was able to feel her trepidation through their Remembrance bond. *"Are you all right?"* he sent mentally to her.

"Yes, Geoffrey," she answered, comforted by his scent that suddenly surrounded her. *"I'm just talking with Malnan."*

The dragon's voice broke through her brooding thoughts. "Now that I have returned to Mynos, dragonkind has a chance to return to its former glory."

Another shiver raced through Arianna when she realized that Mynos and Malnan could indeed populate the skies with dragons once more.

"How wonderful that would be," she said in awe.

"Yes, Daughter, it would. And I believe Mynos is determined to get me pregnant."

"You're probably not too far from the truth!"

The two women giggled on the staircase just as the main doors to the castle creaked open. Sir Ethan and Meghan walked in, closing the door with a resounding thud behind them.

Arianna stood, smoothing her deep blue skirts, and walked toward them.

"Sir Ethan," she called out, her voice echoing off the vaulted ceiling, "so good to see you. Won't you introduce me?"

Ethan smiled as he glanced at his queen and steered

Meghan toward her.

"Queen Arianna, meet Meghan, Sir Duncan's sister."

Meghan's eyes grew wide as Arianna curtseyed and held out her hand. "How do you do, Meghan?"

"Fi-fine, th-thank you, Your Majesty," she stammered, bowing low as she took her hand.

"I trust you've been well taken care of?" Arianna asked, looking to Ethan.

"Oh yes, Your Majesty, she has her own chambers, right down the hall from mine."

"Indeed," Arianna said. "You must watch yourself around this one, Lady Meghan. Sir Ethan is a prankster, and prides himself on wooing a woman."

Meghan smiled up at the man beside her. "Oh really?" she asked. Ethan's cheeks flamed red as he cleared his throat.

"The queen exaggerates," he said behind his hand.

"I think not," came Malnan's amused voice behind Arianna. "She speaks true. I've seen it with my own eyes."

Arianna could hear Meghan's sharp gasp as she gazed at the human form of Mynos's mate.

"Lady Meghan, this is the dragon Malnan," she said, turning to the woman standing behind her.

Meghan clutched onto her stomach as her face turned white.

"My lady?" Ethan asked, a twinge of concern in his voice. "Are you all right?"

She looked up at his face and leaned into him. Ethan's arm wrapped around her and Arianna smiled at the sight.

"I will be fine, Sir Ethan," she said, clutching on to him. "Please, just give me a moment."

"Do not be frightened, Daughter," Malnan said soothingly. "I will not harm you."

Meghan nodded, yet remained within Ethan's embrace.

"Milady, why don't you recite your poem to Malnan and see if she is familiar with it? Since she is here, perhaps we don't need to interrupt the king."

"Oh, Geoffrey adores his interruptions," Arianna said with a grin, laughing even harder when she heard his voice in her head once more.

"You exaggerate, Rose, my love," he said mentally, calling her by the intimate nickname he'd given her when they'd first met. *"I only adore* your *interruptions."*

"Behave, my king," she teased silently.

"Your Majesty?" Ethan asked with a look of confusion.

Arianna waved her hand in front of her face with a smile. "Oh, it's nothing. Now what did you say about a rhyme?"

"My father used to tell my brother and me a rhyme as children, about an evil red ruby. I told it to Sir Ethan and he suggested I let the king know. But...I'm not so sure it's anything more than a child's bedtime story."

Malnan stared at her with her strange, slitted eyes. "A red ruby you say?" she asked in a small voice.

"Yes. It's called the Dragon's Flame."

"Have you heard of it?" Ethan asked.

Malnan shook her head. "I have not heard of the 'Dragon's Flame', but I do know of a red ruby."

Meghan gasped, staring up at Ethan with shock.

"Was this talisman evil, by chance?" he asked.

"Tell me the rhyme, Daughter," Malnan urged, without answering his question.

As Meghan recited it, she blushed under the dragon's intense scrutiny.

"It lies in the Dragon's Death..." Malnan whispered, her eyes wide.

"Malnan?" Arianna said with concern.

The dragon gasped as she covered her mouth with her hand. "This talisman in the rhyme," she whispered in shock, "if it's the same red gem I'm thinking of—I created it!"

Chapter Eight

All eyes in the room were on Meghan as she squirmed in the overstuffed chair in King Geoffrey's study. It was unnerving being stared at not only by two living dragons, but by the king and queen as well. Even Ethan, who was pacing back and forth near the large window, was looking at her intently, waiting for her to speak.

After the dragon divulged that she had created a red gem millennia ago, the queen herself had insisted on an audience with the king, summoning Mynos with her magic. Now everyone was present as they awaited Meghan to once again recite her poem to the group.

Clearing her throat, she licked her lips and willed her voice not to crack as she began the rhyme. After her voice cut through the silence, no one spoke. She chanced a glance at Mynos, who was now looking at his mate. His eyes seemed to darken.

"Malnan, my love," he said, "tell us exactly what you did when you disobeyed me by going to that valley in the Mountains of the Night all those years ago."

Malnan flinched for a moment before she met Mynos's eyes, and then sighed. "I did what I had to do. I consecrated the bodies of the dragons that fell from the skies. I couldn't bear to see our kind killed so easily. I wanted to create a legacy so that no one would forget."

"How many did you make?" His voice was calm, but even from where she sat, Meghan could tell the golden dragon was tense. He must have been referring to the first war for the Crystal millennia ago, when all of dragonkind had fallen on the battlefield in their effort to retrieve the stolen talisman.

"Three."

"You are sure?"

"Yes. I made my lavender jewel, a blue gem and also a red one."

"Are you telling us that there are *two more* talismans unaccounted for?" King Geoffrey interrupted.

"It would seem so, Your Majesty," Mynos said, turning his slitted eyes to him.

An uncomfortable silence descended upon the room, making Meghan fidget once more. Ethan finally stopped his pacing and sat in one of the chairs next to her. He sighed and smoothed his hair back.

"Do you remember *who* you consecrated, Malnan?" Mynos asked.

Malnan closed her eyes as her brow furrowed. After a few moments, she nodded. "Yes. Khrythsan was the dragon I made my lavender jewel from. Qatyanne was the blue. As for the red talisman, that was..."

The dragon lifted her green eyes to her mate's. Tears clearly shone, threatening to fall. "Mynos, forgive me."

Kneeling next to her, he took her hand and kissed her palm. "Tell me who it was, my love."

"Djendorl. It was Djendorl! And I...I remember feeling something when I made that ruby, I remember...weaves of

61

magic that were not my own."

After a moment of silence, Malnan's eyes grew wide. "I know what it was. I didn't have time to think about it then, but now I know."

"What is it?"

"Djendorl wasn't dead. Oh God, Mynos, he wasn't dead when I consecrated his body!"

☙

Meghan gasped as she watched the green dragon weeping on Mynos's shoulder. "What does that mean?" she found the courage to ask.

Mynos turned to her, composing himself before he spoke. "It means, Daughter, that Djendorl's essence would have been trapped in that gem, much like Malnan's soul was pulled into her Jewel. If that is truly what happened, then it only stands to reason this red gem and the Dragon's Flame in your rhyme are one and the same."

"But aren't your talismans blank slates after you create them?" Arianna asked. "Don't they need to be enchanted before they can work magic?"

"Yes, that is true. However, this is different. Malnan's soul could only emerge from her Jewel if she had access to a dragon's egg, which she did. This was because the gem that housed her soul was not made from her own body. Since Djendorl wasn't dead, his soul was trapped in the gem, which *had* been created from his own body. It would therefore allow his soul to manifest itself in anyone who touched it, accounting for the madness described in Lady Meghan's rhyme."

"So anyone who touches this gem will go mad?" Geoffrey

asked, his eyes wide.

Both Mynos and Malnan nodded their heads. "Yes, Your Majesty," Malnan said as she wiped her eyes. "They would take on the lusts and desires of a red dragon."

"Red dragons were among the very worst of our kind," Mynos explained. "Black dragons were also evil in nature, however, their obsession was one of power. Black dragons wanted to rule over as much as they could, whether it be simple farmers, other dragons, or even the entire kingdom."

"Which explains why Iruindyll wanted the Crystal so badly," Arianna whispered.

"Yes, Daughter. But reds, they were particularly nasty. They didn't care about domination or ruling over anyone. Their one and only purpose was destruction. Fire to them was a beautiful thing. Scorched earth and the cries of babies were what they longed for. And Djendorl was the oldest red dragon in the sky. He bided his time and only listened to me out of respect. He secretly longed for the day he could kill me and destroy all I'd come to love."

"Good God!" Ethan exclaimed.

Meghan couldn't stop her body from trembling.

"And yet he respected you?" Geoffrey asked, a confused look on his face.

"Yes, my son. Every dragon respected me. I was their king, after all."

Geoffrey's jaw dropped to the floor. "Their *king*?"

Nodding, Mynos said, "Only gold dragons are the rulers of all dragonkind, as we desire peace and prosperity. Our minds are not clouded by hatred or greed. And yet, only one gold dragon at a time will ever fly in the skies."

"You are the only gold dragon of your kind?" Arianna

asked, her eyes wide.

"Yes, Daughter, then as well as now. Only gold dragons can produce gold dragon offspring, and they are always male. If the time comes for Malnan to bear me a son, he will be gold, and he will be the next ruler of dragonkind, however miniscule that may be."

"So when Iruindyll wanted to be your mate..." Arianna began.

"She wanted not only to rule over humans, but dragons as well. Yes, Daughter, that was her desire."

"Do you know where this gem is?" Geoffrey asked.

Malnan shook her head. "We can start in the valley it was created, however it seems to have been found long enough for this rhyme to circulate. My guess it is no longer there. And yet, it seems to still be somewhere within the Dragon's Death Mountains. According to the rhyme, someone braved the madness to bury it. Perhaps it is in a cave of some kind."

"Can you find it? Can you destroy it?"

Malnan glanced up at King Geoffrey. "That, Your Majesty, is something I do not know."

"But what about this other blue stone?" Ethan said, bringing everyone's thoughts back to the second gem in question. "Where is it?"

At that moment, Geoffrey's sword blazed forth with bright light, buzzing loudly on his hip. Everyone gasped at the unexpectedness of it. Even Geoffrey was taken aback, stumbling a bit.

"What the...Quicksilver?" the king said in confusion. Once he pulled it from its scabbard, its intensity was so bright everyone had to shield their eyes. The white glow of enchantment bathed the room, seemingly brighter than the sun as the sword danced in Geoffrey's hand.

After a few more moments of buzzing, Geoffrey's tear-filled eyes focused on his queen. "Arianna," he whispered, his voice catching.

"What is it, Geoffrey?" she asked, rising from her seat to place her hand on his arm.

Sniffling, Geoffrey covered her hand with his. "Rose, baby..."

"Tell me," she urged, fear etched on her face.

"Your father...Rose, your father had the blue talisman."

"What?" she exclaimed. "But that's not possible! He never had a blue gem, I would have remembered!"

Geoffrey shook his head. "No, he had it. Oh God."

"Geoffrey?" she whispered.

"It's why he left the castle. He figured out how to use it. He took it to his farm and hid it where no one would find it."

"But—"

"Quicksilver is telling me all this...it's telling me..."

With a sob, Geoffrey dropped the weapon. Turning to his wife, he stared at her for a few long, silent moments before Arianna gasped and covered her mouth with her hand.

"That can't be!"

"It's true, Rose. Quicksilver told me it's true!"

"What's wrong?" Ethan wanted to know, damning their Remembrance bond just then.

Another sob ripped through the king as he strode through the study and disappeared out the door. Arianna wasn't too far behind.

"Mynos?" Ethan glanced to the dragon who'd bent to pick up the king's sword. With a sigh, the dragon shook his head after silently conversing with the weapon.

"Geoffrey is correct. Arianna's father did indeed have it. The blue talisman *has* been enchanted. According to the sword, it was found and enchanted by the elves. Sir Isaac of Winterborne learned how to use its magic many years ago, not long after Arianna was born. Unfortunately, the power of the gem killed his best friend, Sir Connor of Emberdale, King Geoffrey's father."

"That's horrible!" Meghan cried as she wiped her eyes. She could barely stop her sobs from escaping, her emotions still raw after learning the truth of the Dragon's Flame. Ethan stood and pulled her into his arms, his warmth comforting her as she clung to him.

"It would seem we need to summon King Kaas for an audience," Mynos whispered, turning his eyes back to his mate. "It was his sister Kendra who gave her eldest son the gem."

"What did they enchant it with?" Ethan wanted to know. "What is its magic?"

"Apparently, Sir Ethan, it can control the weather," Mynos said in awe. "According to Quicksilver, the elves called it the Eye of the Storm."

Chapter Nine

Queen Arianna found her husband sitting in a quiet alcove near the royal apartments. The small window he gazed out of allowed a sliver of sunlight to glint off his blond hair. Her breath caught as she looked at him, still awed by the fact that he loved her deeply.

She could feel his grief through their bond as her tears fell, and she knew he could feel hers as well.

Arianna didn't speak, she merely placed her hand on his shoulder. His body quaked under her fingertips and she drew in a ragged breath. Geoffrey didn't speak as he placed his hand over hers, pulling her into the alcove with him.

Arianna was still reeling from the news that her father had possessed Malnan's blue talisman. But when Geoffrey's tear-filled eyes looked at her, her heart broke for him.

"Geoffrey, I am so sorry," she managed to say past the lump in her throat.

"It's not your fault, Rose," he whispered, drawing her into his embrace.

"But if my father hadn't tried to use the gem, if he hadn't tried to see what it could do, then your father would still be alive."

Geoffrey buried his face into her neck and inhaled deeply. "We cannot regret the actions of others," came his muffled voice. "Your father had no idea that by using it he would cause anyone harm. According to Quicksilver, he tried to conjure a few clouds, but lost control and conjured a nasty thunderstorm instead. *I* was the one who wandered away from camp. *I* was the one my father was trying to find when he fell into that ravine."

"Don't you dare blame yourself," Arianna told him, leaning back to frame his face with her hands. "You were a five-year-old boy. You didn't know any better."

Silence surrounded them as they hugged each other.

After a few moments, Arianna heard Geoffrey's voice in her head. *"Do you think if my father had lived that Sir Isaac would have enchanted us with the Remembrance?"*

Arianna thought about that for a moment. *"I don't know,"* she finally answered him. *"But I can only hope that he would have. I don't know what I'd do without you."*

Geoffrey pressed his lips to hers. It was a gentle kiss until Arianna felt his grip tighten. After what they had both just learned, they needed comfort from one another. She answered his kiss with a passion of her own.

"If we don't get to our apartments soon," Geoffrey's strained voice said in her head, *"I fear I'm going to disgrace the queen of Lyndaria right here in this alcove."*

Arianna smiled at that and pulled away, waving her hand in the air. "Your wish is my command, my lord."

A small magical portal opened in the hallway, leading straight into their bedchamber.

"I am demanding an audience with you, Your Majesty," he said with a suggestive smile. "Right now."

With that, he stepped through the portal and tugged her in

after him. It closed silently behind them.

Cʒ

"Sir Ethan, what have I done?"

"Calm down, milady," he soothed. "You have done nothing."

"But Mynos and the king! Everyone was crying. They were crying because of me." Meghan stopped in the middle of the hallway that led back to her chambers. She'd wanted to lie down after what Malnan had just revealed, but her entire body was trembling and there was nothing she could do to stop it.

"Because of you," Ethan said, tucking a stray lock of her red-gold hair behind her ear, "Mynos and the king finally know about the two other jewels Malnan created so long ago."

"I can't believe it's real," Meghan croaked, holding on to Ethan's strong arms to steady herself. "I can't believe the Dragon's Flame is real! I think I'm going to be sick."

"Then let's get you back to your room, milady," Ethan urged, pulling her along with him as he continued walking.

It didn't take long before they reached her door. Ethan opened it and ushered her inside. Pulling back the blankets on her bed, he indicated for her to lie down.

"You need your rest," he said gently.

Meghan nodded, wanting desperately to ask him to stay with her. But she knew Sir Ethan had his duties to attend to, among other things. He couldn't be with her every hour of the day.

"If you need anything, pull on that sash over there." He pointed to a purple and gold sash hanging from the ceiling. "That will bring the maids to help you. And if you need me, they will be able to find me. Will you be all right?"

Biting her lip, she shuddered as she reached for him. He drew her into his embrace and held her close. She felt protected. Secure. As if his arms were the only safe harbor she had. In her heart of hearts Meghan wished she could hold onto him forever.

When he pulled back, he smiled as he looked into her eyes.

"I know you're scared, Meghan. But nothing will harm you here at the castle. Not only do you have me, but you have all of the king's Wolverines to protect you, not to mention the power of Mynos and Malnan."

She lay back on the pillows and wiped her eyes. "You must think I'm silly."

"Of course not!" he exclaimed. "Why would you think so?"

"I'm a grown woman and yet I jump at shadows."

Cupping her chin, he made her look at him. "You're a grown woman who has just lost her brother and learned that one of her worst childhood nightmares is real. You have every reason to be afraid."

Sniffling, she whispered, "I feel so safe when I'm with you."

Ethan smiled at that. "Then I am doing something right."

He leaned over and kissed her forehead, pulling the blankets around her.

"Rest now, Meghan."

She nodded as he walked away, giving him one last smile before he closed the door gently behind him.

Meghan sighed as she stared at the ceiling. She didn't know how he'd done it, but her body was no longer shaking. Her fears seemed to melt away whenever he smiled at her.

Closing her eyes, she rolled over to get comfortable. The bed was indeed soft and warm. With another small sigh, Meghan realized that in just one day, she'd fallen in love with

Sir Ethan of Krey. How could one man be so wonderful?

Chapter Ten

Lady Jewel of Tabrinth laughed as Ethan bowed low before her in the banquet hall. He made a grand flourish, as if she were royalty, then stood straight once again, his eyes twinkling.

"And to what do I owe this honor?" she asked him, tucking a wisp of her long black hair behind her ear.

"Just that your beauty outshines everyone present, my dear," he told her with a sly grin.

"Now Ethan," she admonished lightly, patting his arm. "You know I'm a married woman." She glanced toward her husband, Sir Sebastian of Tabrinth, Captain of the Guard at Castle Templestone. Her face softened as she watched him talking with King Geoffrey. That pesky lock of hair tumbled into his eyes, making him snap his head back in that old familiar way. Her heart swelled.

"Yes, well, I haven't let it stop me before."

Jewel laughed at that. "You scoundrel!" She gasped in mock horror, knowing full well his flirtation was harmless. Sir Ethan had once indeed tried to win her heart away from his Captain, but the moment it became obvious that she only loved one man, his advances had been more for her husband's benefit than his own. For whatever reason, Ethan loved to plague Sebastian.

"You're not the only woman to tell me so, milady." With that, he lifted her hand and kissed her skin, lingering longer than was necessary.

"Ogling my wife again, are we?" Sebastian's deep voice resonated behind him, making him jump.

"Indeed, Seb," Ethan told him, smiling broadly. "I'm still holding out hope that she will see the error of her ways and fall into my arms."

Sebastian growled at that, scowling at his old friend. "You already have a woman in your life," he said, nodding his head toward the double doors of the hall. "And it looks as if you'll have to explain to her exactly why you were fawning over Jewel."

Ethan turned and glanced at the entry, noticing the stricken look on Meghan's face as she stood there staring back at him. She looked exquisite. The royal-blue velvet of her dress set off her hair, making it shimmer in the light. Pale blue silk highlighted the dress through a split in her skirt and also her long sleeves, while blue embroidery laced her bodice as well. Ethan had never thought it was possible that another woman could take his breath away as the Lady Jewel once had. But before him stood the one woman who'd plagued his thoughts ever since the moment he'd first looked into her eyes.

Now, however, those eyes betrayed the hurt within her as she turned and ran in the other direction.

"Damn!" Ethan dashed after her.

CB

Meghan didn't know where she was going and she didn't care. She raced down a corridor, hearing the shocked gasps of the servants as she passed.

It hadn't been too long ago that she'd awoken from her slumber, and dressed for the evening meal in a stunning blue, crushed velvet dress. She'd worn it for only one reason. To get Sir Ethan's attention.

But it appeared the man already had a woman in mind and it wasn't her. The lady had been lovely, with dark black hair tumbling over her shoulders and a beautiful heart-shaped face. It was no wonder Ethan favored her. She couldn't contend with that, not with her ugly red hair and common ancestry. Surely that striking woman was of noble blood.

Sorrow and anguish ripped through her as she ran, thinking herself a fool for ever harboring tender, hopeful thoughts for Sir Ethan of Krey. She really knew nothing about him. Except that he was considerate and handsome and...amazing.

Crying even harder, she barely noticed the enormous paintings on the walls as she made her way to the closed double doors at the end of the passage. In her desperation, she pushed on one of the doorknobs until the door slowly creaked open into the room beyond.

The sight before her made her gasp.

The magnificent vaulted ceiling of an ornate chapel towered high above her. Deep red carpet covered the floor, muffling her footsteps as she walked up the aisle, trying to get control of her breathing. A few torches and candles lit the room, giving it a warm glow as the darkened stained-glass windows loomed along the walls.

Despite the beauty of the cathedral before her, Meghan's troubled thoughts plagued her. Perhaps now was the time she should go back to Marynville.

"Meghan!" Ethan's deep voice echoed loudly throughout the chapel, making her squeal as she turned to face him. He turned and closed the huge door behind him. It shut with a resounding thud.

"What are you doing in here?" he asked in a gentler voice, approaching her slowly.

She took in a ragged breath and shook her head. "Go away, Sir Ethan."

"No."

"Please?"

"*No.* Not until you tell me why you ran from the banquet hall as if a Dark Knight of Darragh was behind you!"

Meghan turned and walked farther away from him, marching up the aisle. Before she knew he had even moved, Ethan grabbed her arm, stopping her retreat.

"I am a fool," she finally confessed, staring at his chest. "I ran because I thought that you...that you—"

"That I what?" he asked, taking a step closer. When he looked at her like that, she could feel her heart pounding.

Taking a deep breath, she said, "I think it's time I go back to Marynville, Sir Ethan."

"Why?" His voice was firm and loud, demanding an answer.

"I have done what I came here to do. I paid my respects to my brother. I met the king, and even Mynos and Malnan. Because of me, they now know of the Dragon's Flame, and I wish them luck with finding and destroying it. But there is nothing for me here."

"What about our talk earlier? About never leaving?"

"Sir Ethan." She gave him a watery smile. "You can't have two women in your life. You have vowed to protect me, and as such I will think of you as taking Duncan's place. I will rest easy in knowing that you will watch over me. But *she* will not approve of the time you spend with me, nor would I allow it. It's not proper."

"Who are you talking about?"

"Your lady." In saying those words, Meghan covered her eyes and stepped away from him. It hurt too much to be so close, to know he would never be hers. "I must leave."

Meghan had every intention of running again, but as before, Ethan's warm hand stopped her. "I have no lady," he exclaimed.

"Do not deceive me, Sir Ethan, I saw you with her this evening."

"The woman you saw is the Lady Jewel of Tabrinth, wife of Sir Sebastian. I kissed her hand and flirted with her, yes, not because I'm interested in impressing her, but because I enjoy vexing her husband. Seb and I have been friends for a great many years, Lady Meghan. And while I admit I once hoped Lady Jewel would choose me over him, she never did. Now I am quite over her. It was all in good fun, milady, I assure you."

Meghan glanced at the carpet with mixed feelings. If she said one more word, she was sure she'd break into sobs, and she was so tired of crying. Her chest rose and fell as she took in all he had said, trying hard to control her emotions.

"But if I did have a lady," he was saying, his voice suddenly low and soft, "I'd want her to be just like you."

With a gasp, she looked into his eyes and saw no sign of teasing in their brown depths. In fact, what she saw made her shudder for a completely different reason.

Once again, he stepped closer to her, framing her face with his large hands. With sweeping strokes, he wiped the tears from her cheeks with the pads of his thumbs.

"Do not cry," he whispered to her as he lowered his head. "It rips my heart to see you upset. And please, Meghan, don't go. Don't leave the castle."

"But I don't have a reason to stay," she breathed as her heart raced. Ethan was so close, he filled her entire vision.

"Yes, you do." He rubbed her nose with his. Their lips touched, sending shock waves through her entire body. He was gentle and chaste, calming her fears with his tender caress.

After a few moments of surprise, Meghan's heart soared into the sky as she lifted her arms tentatively to his shoulders. He deepened the kiss, angling her head for greater plunder.

Meghan whimpered when his tongue ran the line of her lips, and without any further coaxing, opened her mouth to him. Slowly and masterfully, Ethan delved deep, tasting her, holding her so she couldn't flee him again. She answered his fervor with a passion of her own, surprising herself with her ardor. She didn't want him to stop, she wanted to kiss him for the rest of her life.

Her hands found their way into his hair, releasing it from his leather strap, but he didn't seem to notice—or care.

"You look beautiful tonight." He panted as he pulled away to kiss a path down her neck. "I've never seen a woman more lovely."

She gasped as he lightly bit her beating pulse, her fingers still weaving themselves through his hair.

"I wore this dress for you," she confessed in a small voice. "I wanted you to notice me."

Ethan growled at that and took her mouth again savagely. Before she knew it, Meghan could feel the plush, red carpet underneath her. How had she gotten on the floor? She didn't know and she didn't care. Ethan was kissing her.

"You don't have to wear a pretty dress to get me to notice you," he groaned against her lips. His weight pressing down on her felt heavenly. She pulled him closer, making sure not even a breath separated them.

When she felt him caress her breast through her bodice she gasped and pulled away, looking into his enflamed eyes.

"What's the matter? Am I moving too fast for you?"

"No," she said. "It's just that no man has ever been so...familiar with me before."

He smiled at her. "So it would seem that not only am I charged with protecting your life, but your virginity as well?" His hand still stroked her, puckering her nipple under the fabric and rolling it with his fingers. She gasped at his audacity, then chuckled.

Bolstered by his own crude humor, she decided to pay him back in kind. "I was hoping you'd help me get rid of that annoying little nuisance."

His eyes widened in shock before his loud, delighted laughter echoed off the hallowed walls of the chapel.

Chapter Eleven

"Why, Sir Ethan, have you fallen atop Meghan?"

The voice of the dragon Malnan reverberated throughout the cathedral, shocking Ethan more than he'd care to admit. Jumping off Meghan as if he'd been burned, he offered her his hand and blushed to the roots of his hair.

Clearing his throat, he answered, "Why yes, Malnan, I must have slipped." Glancing back to the woman he'd just been kissing feverishly, he could tell she wanted to be anywhere else at that moment than caught on the floor of the chapel in a compromising position with him. Her eyes were downcast and her cheeks glowed red. She was undeniably beautiful like that and Ethan wished the dragon would just go away.

Malnan gave him a critical stare, her pert mouth curving upwards slowly, telling him all he needed to know. She knew what he'd been up to.

At that moment, Mynos himself appeared through a hole in the wall that Ethan was quite sure hadn't been there just a moment ago. Meghan glanced up and saw it herself, her eyes widening, but she said nothing.

Then understanding hit Ethan full force. There was plenty of talk from the men of the castle that somewhere within the fortress was a secret door that led to Mynos's lair, yet no one knew where it was located. That secret door had to be what he was witnessing now.

"Why are you not at supper, Sir Ethan?" Mynos asked with a grin as he pushed a stone in the wall. A soft click could be heard and the wall rumbled back into place. Ethan's jaw dropped.

"Is that your..."

He didn't get any further. Mynos smiled and nodded. "Yes, Son, this is the portal to my cave under the castle. Long ago, only the kings of Lyndaria knew of this door. Now, a select few are aware of it. I trust you will keep my secret?"

Ethan bowed slightly as he inclined his head. "Of course, Mynos."

Meghan stared at the dragons and timidly took Ethan's hand. He pulled her close, glancing around on the floor for the leather strap that held back his hair. Without it, his hair tumbled down around his face. He ran his fingers through it and sighed, knowing there was no hope of finding it now.

"Are you all right, Daughter?" Malnan asked, apparently noting Meghan's pink cheeks.

She nodded furiously, keeping her eyes averted and squeezing Ethan's hand so tight he winced.

"Well, I suppose we should be getting back to the banquet hall," he said. "If you will excuse us?"

Both Mynos and Malnan inclined their heads. Ethan turned and led Meghan out of the chapel.

"It seems as if those two have the right idea," Mynos said softly after a few moments of silence, wrapping his arms around his mate from behind.

"And what might that be?" Malnan asked, not at all feeling as calm as she sounded. The touch of Mynos's hands always made her shiver, and now was no exception.

"Indulging in their passion."

His heady words made her lean her head back on his strong shoulder. "Shouldn't we make an appearance at the banquet?"

Mynos began kissing the tender skin of her neck. "Indeed we should, my love." His hands became bolder, roaming up and down her human form with an expertise only he possessed.

"Mynos, someone will see!" she exclaimed.

With a flick of his wrist, Malnan could feel the weaves of magic in the air. She knew what he'd just done. He'd magically locked the doors to the chapel. They wouldn't budge unless he wished it.

"You were saying?"

"You are insatiable!" she panted, finally allowing herself to feel his passion.

"I've been without you for millennia, Malnan," he whispered into her ear. "I intend to make up for lost time."

Turning in his arms, Malnan surrendered to him as he lowered her to the floor. Her soft gasps echoed, not only off the walls of the cathedral, but also through the thundering heart of the mighty golden dragon.

03

Sir Ethan hadn't let go of Meghan's hand since he'd practically sprinted from the chapel. He led her through the hallways until they came to the servant's stairs.

"This way, milady," he said, pulling her along behind him.

"Where are we going?" she asked. "Shouldn't we return to the banquet hall?"

Once they reached the top of the steps, Ethan found an alcove on the wall and pressed her into the shadows.

"Your dress is hopelessly wrinkled and my hair loose when I never wear it so. Do you think the patrons of the banquet hall will not know what we've been about?"

Meghan shuddered at his nearness, losing herself in his brown eyes. She had wondered what he looked like with his hair down and now she knew. Ethan was even more handsome than she could have imagined with soft, sandy-colored hair falling to his shoulders in waves. Without thinking of what she was doing, Meghan reached up and threaded her fingers through it.

"I like you this way," she whispered, glancing over his shoulders to make sure no one was near.

The smile he graced her with took her breath away. "Should I do away with my leather strap altogether?" he asked her, quirking a brow as he leaned in closer.

"Without a doubt, Sir Ethan," she said softly, standing on her toes to whisper her words in his ear. She could feel his body shiver from her breath alone and she couldn't help but smile in delight.

Turning his face to hers, he lowered his lips as if to kiss her once more, but voices down the passage interrupted them.

"Damn," he swore, pulling away from her.

"What?"

"Unless you want an audience, I should take you back to your chambers." Holding his arm out for her, he waited until she accepted it before he began to lead her down the hall.

"And these are the servants' quarters, milady," he said loudly as they passed two maids with arms full of dirty linens. It was all Meghan could do to contain her laughter at the look of utter confusion on the women's faces as they passed.

Once they were out of earshot, she giggled. "Sir Ethan!"

"What?" he asked with a perfectly innocent look on his face. "How else were we to explain why a knight and a guest of the king were roaming about where we shouldn't have been?"

Meghan laughed even harder. "You are outlandish!"

"I try, milady, believe me I do." With a wink and a smile, he led her all the way back to her own room.

"I will order some food to be brought up for us," he said, opening the door for her. "That is, if you don't mind dining alone with me. In your quarters."

The teasing light in his eye made Meghan blush. "Haven't we been scandalous enough for this evening, my lord?"

With a devilish grin, Ethan kissed her hand. "Scandalous? Why, milady Meghan, you have yet to see scandalous."

With that, he turned and walked down the hall, intent on finding some food. Meghan closed the door and leaned against it, her heart slamming against her chest. Never in her life had she been so forward with a man. Sir Ethan was intense, threatening to make her beg for her own surrender.

Could she handle him? She didn't know and the thought almost scared her enough to lock her door. But her body ached to feel his hands on her again and yearned for his lips to kiss her skin. Perhaps it wasn't the brightest idea she'd ever had, dining alone in her room with a virile, sexy man. But she realized she didn't care.

If Sir Ethan of Krey wanted to lay siege to her body, she wasn't about to stop him. She just hoped that while he was storming her defenses, she could capture his heart.

Chapter Twelve

As Ethan entered the kitchens, he grinned when he saw Sir Sebastian leaning on a chopping block. The cooks were almost comical, trying not to fall over themselves to get a tray of food ready for the Captain of the Guard. Mistress Wynette barked orders here and there, filling a tray with the fare from the banquet hall.

Leaning next to him, Ethan chuckled. "So it would seem we both have the same idea."

Sebastian gave him a fleeting, sidelong glance, and then turned his head again to stare in shock.

"Why, Ethan, is this a new look for you?"

Running his fingers through his unbound hair, Ethan couldn't help but smile. "Meghan prefers my hair down. What can I say?"

Sebastian's bark of laughter rang through the kitchens. "So soon you are doing her bidding?"

"She is a wonderful girl who's lost her only family. If she wants me to wear my hair down, then I will do it."

"Very noble of you," Sebastian said, a twinkle in his eye.

"What are you doing in the kitchens? Didn't I just see you in the banquet hall with Lady Jewel?"

"Indeed you did, but my wife isn't feeling well. She asked to dine in our apartments. Her pregnancy isn't quite agreeing with her at the moment."

Ethan nodded, a twinge of jealousy pulsing through him. With the mention of his Captain's pregnant wife, he realized just how badly he wanted that for himself. A family. Stability for his future. He suddenly thought what Meghan might look like, her belly round with his child, smiling at him as his wife. His heart swelled. An ache settled in his stomach.

Meghan seemed to accept his advances, and even shocked him with her playful banter. She was so glorious and innocent, that he knew he wanted her all to himself. He'd endeavor to make her his.

"I spoke with Geoffrey before I left the banquet." Sebastian's voice broke into Ethan's thoughts.

"Oh?"

"He wants me to pick a few of my men to go to Arianna's old farm and search for the Eye of the Storm, Malnan's blue talisman. They're to leave tomorrow."

"Who did you pick?" Ethan asked, grabbing a small carrot off Sebastian's tray and popping it into his mouth.

"Cederick will be going."

Ethan nodded. "Good choice."

"And you."

Stopping in mid-chew, he felt his skin prickling. "Me?"

"Ethan, you're one of my best men. And you won't be gone long."

He swallowed the carrot, no longer feeling like eating. When one of the cooks handed him his tray, he held it but didn't budge.

"She will be just fine," Sebastian said, trying to placate his friend by placing a hand on his shoulder. "You have my word on that."

"I know," Ethan said softly.

"You are Meghan's protector, Ethan, but you are also a Wolverine. You cannot dismiss your duty to the king."

"She's just so scared. I don't know how to tell her I'll be leaving. And so soon!"

"Don't worry about it," Seb said with a wide grin. "If all goes well, you'll be back in her arms before sunset." With that, he winked and lifted his tray, exiting the kitchen.

Ethan sighed as he watched him go. He hoped Sebastian was right. And he hoped Meghan would understand why he had to leave her.

Scowling, he made his way back to her chambers, dinner tray in hand.

CB

Meghan moved to open the door when she heard a soft knock on the other side. She'd taken off her voluminous blue gown and donned a simple pale yellow robe that covered her undergarments quite nicely. She wanted something to cover her body, but not anything that would be too complicated to get off if Ethan had other things on his mind. Just that thought alone had her blushing as her hands trembled. She wondered if total surrender to Ethan was the best thing for her to do.

While she had brushed the tangles from her long red hair, she remembered kissing Ethan earlier and her entire body tightened with anticipation. She'd never felt this way about a man before and it scared her. Never had Meghan thought she'd feel something so powerful so fast. She felt as if she'd lived a lifetime since she met Ethan, not barely more than a day.

Perhaps giving herself to him now wasn't a good idea. Perhaps she should send him away and claim to have a headache. But the knock on the door was persistent, as was her growling belly, and she knew she couldn't be a coward. She wanted Sir Ethan to be her first lover, however she wasn't sure if she was quite ready to take that big a step with him. Meghan's second thoughts plagued her as she looked down at her robe, and she cursed herself for wearing such revealing attire.

She swallowed hard and opened the door, trying to hide her body behind the thick wood. But one look at Ethan's face made her forget her modesty.

"What is the matter, milord?" she asked him.

Without asking for an invitation, Ethan strode into the room with the food-laden tray and set it on the bed. "I've just come from chatting with Sir Sebastian," he said as he turned. Meghan could hear his gasp even from where she was standing across the room.

"My God, milady, you will make this difficult," he told her, looking her up and down.

Meghan blushed and glanced at the floor, trying to cover herself with her arms crossed on her chest. "Make what difficult?"

With a harsh sigh, Ethan crossed the room to her. She finally found the courage to look at him. His eyes bored into hers. He wanted her. She could see the truth of it plain as day in his dark brown depths.

"I'm leaving in the morning."

His soft words shuddered through her, making her heart flutter inside her. Leaving in the morning? Meghan's eyes grew wide at the realization that he wasn't planning on leaving her room until dawn. He *did* want to spend the night with her. The intense look in his eyes seemed to confirm her thoughts. How could she dissuade him without hurting his feelings? How could she push him away without thoroughly wounding his male pride? She was in love with him, after all, however she didn't feel ready to take the final step that would bring her within the circle of his arms.

"Sir Ethan, I don't think that's such a good idea."

A look of confusion crossed his face.

Licking her lips, she continued. "I...I'm not ready for this. You are an amazing man, please don't get me wrong. And I do want to, but I'd like...that is, maybe we shouldn't move so fast."

Ethan stared at her for a few silent moments before mischief lit in his eyes. He gave her a slow grin. "Lady Meghan, what are you talking about?"

Now it was her turn to be confused. "Well...what are *you* talking about?" she countered.

"I'm leaving the *castle* in the morning, my lady. The king has demanded the Eye of the Storm be found. I'm assuming he wants the Dragon's Flame found as well. But Sebastian is sending Sir Cederick and me to Queen Arianna's old farm house to find where her father hid it."

"Oh." Suddenly Meghan's heart was pounding for a different reason. An irrational fear gripped her.

"Do not worry yourself, milady. Seb has told me it shouldn't take long. I will have the Emerald of Estriel and I might even return before the sun sets."

Meghan simply nodded, her head whirling. Why did she suddenly feel as if her world was spiraling out of control? Ethan was a knight of the king, she knew he had duties that must be attended to. But knowing they had to be separated, even for a short time, weighed heavily on her nerves.

"Can you promise me you'll come back by sunset?"

Ethan looked deep into her eyes and gave her a gentle smile. Reaching up, he stroked her cheek before sliding his fingers through her red-gold waves.

"Unfortunately I cannot make that promise. We will be on this mission until the blue gem is found. If it is not as easy as I hope, then there is a possibility I may be gone for a while."

Meghan tried to keep the fear from her face but failed miserably. Lowering her eyes, she stared at his chest as if it were the most interesting thing in all the world. She felt like such a child, fearing his departure, when she'd lived all alone in her family's cottage for years. What was the matter with her?

"I need to prepare for my journey tonight, milady," he said gently, hooking his finger under her chin. Her eyes met his once again. "I'm afraid I cannot dine with you as I had intended."

Swallowing hard, she nodded at his words.

"Oh, Meghan," he groaned, crushing her to him.

"I will miss you," she said, sniffling into his shoulder.

"And I you."

"Please promise me one thing, Sir Ethan?"

"What is that?"

"Promise you'll come back to me safe. Unharmed."

"Only if you promise me the same," he answered.

She smiled and he smiled back, lowering his head for a chaste kiss. But the moment their lips touched, Meghan locked her hands in his hair, holding him close. She fit him perfectly, curving into his body without the poofy skirts she'd worn before. She whimpered into his mouth as his tongue dipped inside, tasting her. Meghan stood on her toes to press even closer.

"Milady," he groaned against her lips. "Meghan."

"What?" she said breathlessly as he pulled away to kiss her cheeks.

"Keep kissing me like that and I will no longer be responsible for what I do."

"Are you telling me you won't behave like a gentleman?" she teased.

"My sweet woman, I have never claimed to *be* a gentleman."

Meghan chuckled, stroking the skin of his neck. "No you haven't. But you *are* a knight. A girl might simply assume."

"All the more reason to take advantage of that misconception."

"You *are* a scoundrel!" she said with a grin as she smacked his shoulder.

"Indeed I am. Perhaps you should keep your distance."

"Keep my distance?" she said with mock horror. "From my handsome Wolverine?"

"*Your* Wolverine?" he repeated with some shock.

"Yes, mine," Meghan whispered, touching his cheek with the pads of her fingers. "You have vowed to protect me, to keep me from harm, have you not?"

"I have, but—"

"Then you are mine."

A long silence stretched on between them as Meghan's cheeks heated. Ethan smiled. "How can I possibly contend with your logic?"

"You cannot, milord."

"Indeed, I cannot," he confessed, giving her another kiss she felt clear to her toes. "But now I fear your handsome Wolverine must leave you to make preparations for his journey."

Meghan nodded, stroking his cheek once more. "I will still

be here when you return."

"Oh, I'm counting on it, milady. Most eagerly."

Chapter Thirteen

"We have known about the Dragon's Flame and the Eye of the Storm for quite some time now, Your Majesty."

King Kaas of the elves sat in one of the overstuffed chairs in Geoffrey's study, watching the young monarch through steepled fingers. He had just arrived at the castle, making the servants rouse King Geoffrey, just as he'd ordered. The early morning sun was beginning to peek over the horizon, bathing the endless waves of the ocean with gold.

Geoffrey turned slowly from the view of the large window to stare at the elf seated a few feet away. Mynos stood near Geoffrey's desk with his human arm draped across Malnan's shoulder. Kaas's royal escort, Rowan, sat next to the elven sovereign. Sir Cederick leaned against the far wall, holding close to him his elven wife, Meliena, who was nodding at King Kaas's words. Ethan stood just inside the door, having only arrived a few minutes after the elven king. He glanced at Geoffrey and noticed the look of confusion cross his king's features. Ethan clutched the satchel he had prepared for his journey until his knuckles were white.

"How is it that the elves knew of these talismans?" Geoffrey asked.

"Because we found them." Kaas leaned forward in his chair and gave Geoffrey a small grin. "Some of our magic users believe the valley in the Mountains of the Night is still charged with magic, even after these many millennia. A few of them have been known to pilgrimage there."

"The Mountains of the Night?" Cederick asked, looking around from face to face.

"The Dragon's Death Mountains, Son," Mynos said with despair in his eyes. "After the first war for my Crystal, the people of Lyndaria renamed the mountain range, first named after their rich, black soil. It was where we dragons met our untimely end. Thus, the mountains were renamed the Dragon's Death. Only creatures old enough to remember still call the range by its true name."

Cederick nodded. "I believe I have heard that before."

King Geoffrey glanced back to Kaas. "Your mages journey to this valley?"

"Yes. It was during one of these pilgrimages that Keah, one of our most gifted mages, found the blue stone. She brought it back to the palace and presented it to the king. We all knew what it was. It was no accident that the talisman of a dragon was lying on the very same battlefield where all of dragonkind died. But a mere examination determined the stone had yet to be enchanted.

"That year was a hard year for our kingdom. Drought was far and wide. Not only with the elves, but here in Lyndaria as well. King Benjamin had quite the responsibility to make sure his subjects could find sources of water. So Keah had a thought. She took the blue gem and enchanted it as a talisman to control the weather. She then named it the Eye of the Storm. After its creation, she used its magic, and no longer was the land in drought.

"But at that time, tensions between the elves and humans were high, Majesty." Kaas returned Geoffrey's gaze. "We did not tell King Benjamin, nor any of his subjects, about the enchantment of this gem. For all they knew, the rain was sent by God. A miracle. But we elves knew better.

"However, Keah suddenly took ill and died shortly thereafter. Unfortunately, the secret to wielding the magic of the stone seemed to die with her. Many tried, but simply could not tap into her magic weaves. Apparently, in order to safeguard the talisman from being misused, she had also enchanted it with a spell."

"What spell is that?" Geoffrey wanted to know.

"That only members of her own family would be able to wield its power, no one else."

"So it cannot be used by just anyone with a talent for magic?"

"No, Your Majesty."

"Then how did Kendra end up with the stone?"

Kaas's mouth turned up with a faint grin. "Keah was my grandmother."

Geoffrey reached for his chair and stumbled into it. "She was the elven *queen*?"

"Indeed. And she gave the talisman to Kendra when my sister was but a child, before she met Sir Darryn. There hadn't been a harsh drought since the Eye was first enchanted, and therefore, the power of the gem was no longer needed.

"When my sister abdicated her throne to me, much to the shock of the entire royal court, the stone was all but forgotten. Our father demanded that Kendra be banished from the elves for loving a human more than her kingdom. And so she left— but she left with the Eye.

"She didn't take it maliciously, nor did she have any intentions of using it as it was meant to be used. But

94

Grandmother had given it to her, and it was the only thing left that connected her to her former life.

"She and Sir Darryn then had three boys. Kendra had hoped to have a girl, but she did not get her wish. However, she knew her strong magic flowed through both Isaac and Rowan. Since Isaac was the eldest, he was given the talisman."

"And he figured out how to use it," Geoffrey said in a quiet voice.

"Yes, he did," Rowan answered, getting Geoffrey's attention. Arianna's uncle cleared his throat. "The moment the unnatural storm broke out that killed your father, I knew Isaac had learned how to harness its power. I could feel the magical shock waves it created. But after that, he was terrified of using it again. He told me as much. So he left the castle after enchanting you and Arianna with the Remembrance as he and your father, Sir Connor, had once planned.

"Ever since then, he denounced his elven heritage. He refused to use magic and was determined to make his living off the land. He couldn't continue to be a Wolverine, not when he'd killed his closest friend by using the Eye of the Storm."

Geoffrey turned away, his eyes glassy.

"I'm sorry, Your Majesty. Shall I stop?"

"No, no. Continue, Rowan, please."

Nodding once, Rowan took another breath. "Isaac bought a farm near the village of Stollinshire and hid the Eye on his property. He made sure both Seth and I were aware of where it was hidden, in case something should happen. But because he'd denounced his elven heritage, looking at me was too painful for him. My brothers could pass for human. I, on the other hand, could not. My features gave me away. Isaac asked me not to return to the farm. I thought for sure I'd never see my family again."

"Good God, Rowan! And you just accepted that?" Ethan's shocked gasp filled the room.

"What else could I do?" Rowan turned to gaze to the young Wolverine. "My older brother had turned his back on me. Seth almost came with me when I left. However, he'd met a young lady from the village. They soon married and had themselves a daughter."

"Meiri," Geoffrey said softly.

"Yes. Meiri. In order to ignore the pain of never seeing my family again, I sought out the elves. Once I made it known to King Kaas that we were related, we have been friends ever since. He asked me to be his royal escort and I could not refuse."

"Seth is now living back at Arianna's old farmhouse," Geoffrey mused. "He rebuilt the farm and is working the land again."

"Yes, Sire, he is."

"Would he be willing to help Sir Cederick and Sir Ethan retrieve the Eye of the Storm?"

Rowan smiled. "That will not be necessary."

"Why not?"

"Because when I escorted Seth back to Isaac's old farm after your wedding to our niece, he gave the gem to me."

Geoffrey rose out of his seat so fast the chair almost fell over.

"*You* have it?"

Rowan nodded as he reached into a pouch on his belt. "Seth told me the Eye of the Storm should be given back to the royal house of the elves, not tucked away in secret."

With that, Rowan pulled out a magnificent, square-shaped sapphire that winked with a pale blue light. Every eye in the room widened at the sight, while Quicksilver hummed excitedly on Geoffrey's hip.

Ethan dropped his satchel to the floor in stunned silence.

Malnan burst into tears.

⌇

The room was silent, except for Malnan's muffled sobbing as she wept on Mynos's shoulder. Swallowing hard, Geoffrey finally held out his hand.

"May I?" he asked in a shaky voice.

"Of course," Rowan said with a small nod, handing the king the luminous blue gem.

It wasn't heavy as it fit snugly in the palm of his hand. Geoffrey couldn't help the moisture that sprang into his eyes as he held it, both marveling at its beauty, yet fearing its power.

"You say only descendents from Queen Keah can wield the Eye's magic?" he asked in a small voice.

"That is correct," Kaas answered with a slow nod.

"Then that means my wife..."

"And any children you may have with her will have the power. Yes, Your Majesty. Rowan and I also possess the power, as well as Arianna's uncle Seth."

"Are there any others?"

"No others, Sire," Rowan answered. "Kaas's daughter, Princess Derekah, and her son Prince Ryon would have been able to as well, however, they are . . ."

Reaching out, Geoffrey squeezed Rowan's shoulder in understanding. "Yes, we know," he whispered.

"We no longer have to leave?" Cederick asked, his eyes

lighting up as he gazed down at his wife. She blushed, but returned his bold perusal.

"Let's not assume that, Cederick," Geoffrey said, still gripping the Eye of the Storm in his fist. "The Dragon's Flame is out there somewhere." His gaze returned to the elven king. "You wouldn't happen to know where that talisman is, would you?"

With a sigh, Kaas bowed his head. "Unfortunately, yes I do."

Malnan gasped, her tears finally dry.

"Why is that unfortunate?" she asked.

"Because the Dragon's Flame is hideously powerful. It was not enchanted, Your Majesty, however it did have an unholy magic."

"Yes, Malnan has told us as much. The essence of a dragon named Djendorl was trapped inside the gem upon his consecration."

"Whatever you can imagine about this stone, Majesty, it's hundreds of times worse. From the moment our mages found it on the battlefield in that valley, we were plagued with men bent on death and destruction. Each mage thought they could tame the gem, enchant it with some power for good, but their enchantments were only twisted by the soul of the dragon inside, serving to make the madness in its victims that much more severe.

"It didn't take long before our mages realized the Dragon's Flame needed to be destroyed. However, only very strong magic wielded through another draconic talisman could destroy it. Yet, the only other talisman we had was the Eye of the Storm. And a mere rainstorm, even a cataclysmic one, would not be enough to destroy the Flame. We needed the Crystal of Mynos, but it was hidden away, and Mynos had entombed himself in stone. We were helpless against it."

"What did you do?" Ethan asked, walking farther into the room.

"We buried it. Deep within the earth under the Mountains of the Night."

"But how is that possible if anyone who touches it goes mad?" Cederick asked.

Remembering Meghan's poem, Geoffrey said, "One of your mages braved that madness, didn't they, Your Majesty?"

Kaas looked at him and nodded once. "You are correct. One of our strongest mages thought he could take the Flame through a portal and all would return to normal. Even though he enchanted himself with anti-magic spells and the like, he was still consumed by the lust of the Flame. He did indeed cross over to the other side of the portal, a huge cavern we had fashioned under the mountains with no entrance or exit, but we had to leave him there. There was no hope for him. He was buried along with the gem."

"Well, now we have both Mynos and Malnan, as well as the power of the Crystal. We cannot afford to have the Dragon's Flame hidden somewhere underneath those mountains. It is too dangerous. It must be destroyed before it is accidentally found again." Geoffrey squared his shoulders.

"Yes, you are correct. The risk is too great."

"Can you open another portal to this cave?" King Geoffrey wanted to know.

Kaas swallowed hard. "Yes. However, we must be prepared to destroy the Flame before that is attempted. Our legends speak of the Dragon's Flame calling out to you. If someone is not well-versed in magic, there is a high risk they will touch the stone."

Geoffrey's eyes went wide. "Well then. Mynos, Malnan, go and find this Dragon's Flame and destroy it. Take your Crystal.

You will need it."

Mynos bowed and grabbed Malnan's hand. "We will be ready to leave shortly."

"I'm going with you," Rowan said. Silence was his answer.

"If you are coming, Son, then you will need this," Mynos replied, walking over to him. The dragon held out his hand and with a bright flash of light, the Emerald of Estriel appeared, resting in his human palm. "If anything should happen to me or to Malnan, use it to send for help."

Rowan stared at the green talisman in Mynos's hand before he gingerly took it from him. "Let's pray it does not come to that, friend."

"Indeed."

"What should be done with the Eye of the Storm?" Geoffrey asked Kaas.

The elven king rose from his chair and stood in front of him. "Keep it. Your kingdom and mine will one day stand united. It belongs to both the royal house of the elves as well as the royal house of Lyndaria. Someday, Geoffrey, both titles will belong to you and Queen Arianna. All I ask is that you keep it safe."

Geoffrey's hands shook as he nodded, still clutching firmly onto the glittering jewel. "You have my word," he whispered.

Chapter Fourteen

Meghan stretched as sunlight streamed into her room. She lay against her pillows and sighed, saddened at the thought of being separated from Ethan. Now that she was alone at the castle, she had no idea what to do. Where should she go? Perhaps a walk around the grounds would do her some good. Clear her head.

She bounded out of bed and was crossing the room to her bureau when a knock sounded at the door.

"Who is it?"

"It's...Samantha, milady," came the high-pitched voice from the other side of the door. Meghan smiled. Samantha was a maid at the castle, and one of the women who'd helped her with her bath the night before. It would be nice to talk to another woman, and perhaps Samantha could walk with her for a bit.

"Come in," she called out, opening the bureau door. Rifling through the dresses, she heard the door open and close behind her. She chose a lovely peach-colored gown and pulled it down.

"I was thinking about going for a walk today, Samantha," she said. "Would you like to come?"

Without warning, a strong pair of arms caught her from behind and twirled her about the room as she shrieked in surprise.

"Sounds wonderful, milady!" a familiar deep voice resonated throughout the room.

"Sir Ethan!" she exclaimed in shock. "What are you doing in here? Put me down! Where is Samantha?"

With a hearty laugh, Ethan set her on her feet and looked her up and down. It was at that moment she realized she was in nothing more than her bedclothes. Not even her thin yellow robe covered her this time. Her cheeks flamed.

With mock indignation, she crossed her arms on her chest and stared at him.

"'Twas only me at the door, sweet Meghan," he said with a sly grin. "I was hoping to catch a glimpse of you like this."

"Oh!" she gasped, stomping her foot. Crossing the room regally, she grabbed her robe off the back of a chair and donned it. As she tied the belt around her waist, she turned to look at him in confusion.

"Aren't you supposed to be leaving to find the Eye of the Storm? Shouldn't you be gone already?"

"That's what I came to tell you, milady," he said with a sweeping bow. "I no longer have to go. King Kaas himself was in possession of the Eye and brought it with him to the castle. Mynos and Malnan have also just left about an hour ago in search of the Dragon's Flame, to destroy it. Therefore the king had no reason for me to leave the castle."

Understanding dawned on her. "So the king now has the Eye of the Storm?"

"Yes."

"And the dragons have left in search of the red talisman?"

"Yes."

"You're not leaving?" she suddenly yelped, her eyes wide.

He shook his head. "No, I'm not leaving."

Meghan ran across the room and jumped into his arms, making Ethan stagger back with a chuckle. "Oh, thank goodness!" she cried.

"You sure do know how to make a man feel special," he whispered in her ear as he gave her a squeeze.

"But, Sir Ethan," she said as she pulled back to look into his eyes, "you *are* special." Lifting her hand, she stroked his cheek.

"I have a confession to make, milady."

"What is that?"

"I am glad I am not going. I am quite content to stay right where I am."

Meghan giggled at that, as he was in her arms at the moment. "Toss your dice right, Sir Ethan, and you just might stay here," she told him, arching a brow suggestively.

"Is that so?" he countered.

With a slow, deliberate nod, Meghan stood on tip-toe and gave him a soft, chaste kiss. "Now, however, you need to leave."

"Leave?" he said, giving her a wounded look.

"I'm not going to dress in front of you, Sir Ethan, no matter how special you are."

Releasing her, he gave her a playful scowl. "If you insist. However, I'll be just outside in the hall, as I have every intention of showing you around the castle this day, Lady Meghan. Do not make me wait long."

With a wink, he strode to her door and closed it silently behind him. Meghan smiled to herself. He wasn't leaving. She could hardly contain her giddy heart.

$\mathcal{CB}$

"It is so beautiful up here." Meghan took a deep breath and gazed out upon the open ocean. Ethan had led her to the top of the battlements after they finished their breakfast in the kitchens. Glancing over the thick stone wall, Meghan could see the pounding surf that crashed against the rocks far below the cliffs.

A light breeze ruffled her hair, and she tried in vain to tuck her loose tendrils behind her ears—her braid was no match for the gentle wind. When she didn't immediately get a response from Ethan, she turned to look at him, leaning against the wall.

He was staring at her with a handsome smile on his lips.

"Indeed, milady." His deep voice sent shivers down her spine. "It is beautiful up here. *Very* beautiful."

Meghan couldn't hide her blush, but she did not break eye contact with him. He seemed just about to straighten and pull her closer when a loud voice interrupted him.

"Ethan!"

He turned at the sound of his name, and Meghan could have sworn she heard him groan. A handsome man with dark hair and unusual lavender-colored eyes strode up to them with a wide grin on his face. He was about as tall as Ethan, and yet he didn't wear the familiar sword of a Wolverine. In fact, his clothing was made of the finest blue silks and deep red velvets.

"Wonderful to see you, my good man," he said, his rich voice carrying on the breeze. "Aren't you going to introduce me to your lady friend?"

"Why no, I wasn't planning on it."

Meghan gasped at Ethan's sudden prickly demeanor. He moved to step in front of her, as if shielding her from the handsome man.

The man merely laughed and stepped around him, holding out his hand. "I'm Lord Galen of Evendria, milady, and you are?"

"I'm Meghan. Of...of Marynville," she stammered, glancing at Ethan. "Nice to meet you, milord." She began to reach for Galen's offered hand in greeting, but Ethan's own hand snaked out and tucked her fingers underneath his arm before she had the chance.

"This is Lady Jewel's brother, Meghan," Ethan said casually, as if he hadn't just offended the lord standing before him. "He won't be staying long at the castle, I'm afraid. He was only here to attend his sister's 'proper' wedding to Sir Sebastian, which he and his father insisted upon, by the way, even though the Lady Jewel and Sebastian had already been married. But since that 'proper' wedding took place a few days ago, Lord Galen will be leaving Castle Templestone to return to Evendria. Sooner rather than later, I hope, milord?"

Lord Galen was grinning from ear to ear. Meghan couldn't believe it. Ethan was deliberately provoking him.

"Why, Sir Ethan, I've never seen you so...overbearing before," he said, obviously enjoying himself.

"Yes, well, Meghan is Sir Duncan's sister, and she has been given into my care. Your short stay here at the castle has been quite entertaining, to say the least, Galen. I swear you must have every maid and female servant swooning at the sight of you. But forgive me for saving milady Meghan from your charms. I do not want her similarly corrupted."

Galen nodded his head and looked at Meghan thoughtfully. "It would seem to me you just don't want any competition for the lady's attentions. Ironic, wouldn't you say, considering your pursuit of my sister?"

Meghan could feel Ethan's muscles tense as her hand still

rested on his arm. The air was suddenly thick with tension.

"I am sorry, Lord Galen," she found herself saying, "but I do believe you are mistaken in your belief that there could be any competition for my attention. I simply could not fancy a man other than Sir Ethan if I tried. I apologize, but that is the way of it."

Ethan's delighted peals of laughter echoed off the surrounding battlements.

"And you say *I* corrupt the ladies, my good man?" Lord Galen chuckled, smacking Ethan on the shoulder. He glanced back to Meghan and winked at her. "Fair enough, milady. Good day."

With that, he turned on his heel and strode away.

ᬃ

"Why Meghan, you are my champion!"

Ethan had to wipe away his tears of mirth as he laughed heartily. Never in his life had a woman stood up for him in front of a potential rival and it warmed his heart. Meghan was indeed an unpredictable woman, exactly the kind of woman he needed in his life. He just hoped her supposed feelings for him were far deeper than a mere infatuation. Ethan didn't know what he'd do if Meghan left him to make a life with another man.

His thoughts suddenly stopped cold. Here he was, thinking about spending his life with this woman, and he hadn't known her for more than a few days. Not only that, but they hadn't even made love. However, that was a problem he was most intent on solving. The fact that Meghan was now holding his hand gave him hope that she'd be willing to take their little affair to the next level.

He didn't know how he had resisted her earlier that morning when he'd pretended to be the maid just to see her in her nightclothes. Every curve of her body had shown itself to him and his own body had instantly responded. Thank goodness Meghan was too innocent to realize exactly what she was doing to him. Just being near her, touching her, smelling her sweet scent, had Ethan wanting to find a secluded corner in which to ravish her.

"I am no champion, Sir Ethan." Her voice pierced his thoughts. "I merely wanted to make it known that I'm not interested in his advances, if that was his agenda."

"Oh it was, milady, believe me." Ethan rolled his eyes. He walked with her along the battlements, leading her toward the courtyard of the castle. "Lord Galen is more of a womanizer than..."

"Than who? Than you?"

Ethan's head snapped around to look into her smiling eyes.

Meghan cocked her head. "That *is* what you were going to say, wasn't it?"

"Well, perhaps. But those days are behind me."

"Oh?"

Nodding, he smiled at her. "I am tired of chasing skirts and heated trysts. I want stability, I want a future, a family."

"How many...trysts have you had?" Meghan's gaze dropped to her feet as they walked.

"In truth? I do not know, milady."

An uncomfortable silence spread out before them.

"However, Meghan," he said, stopping their stroll and turning toward her, "*You* are not one of them."

She gazed at him, her green eyes shining, and he knew what she wanted to hear.

"You are not a tryst, milady. You are something special, more solid. I have never felt this way about anyone, not even when I was chasing after Lady Jewel. Whatever is happening between us, Meghan, it's genuine. You can count on that."

"What *is* happening between us, Sir Ethan?" Her chin trembled.

"Something wonderful." Leaning over her, he framed her face in his hands and kissed her gently. He didn't care who might see them, he only cared about the soft, warm woman in his arms. He hadn't worn his hair back since their first kiss, and he groaned as he felt her fingers threading through the length of it. When her tongue touched his lips, asking for entrance, his arms tightened around her, never wanting to let go.

He opened for her, kissing her slowly, allowing her to slip her tongue into his mouth. The silken feel of it was almost his undoing.

Pulling away, he hugged her tight, panting hard.

"We need to stop, Meghan," he whispered in her ear. "It is not proper to be so intimate on the top of the battlements."

"Since when have you worried about propriety?" she teased, her own voice a mere whisper.

"Only for your sake, milady," he said. "I am sure you have no secret desire to be made love to on the outer walls of the castle in front of the king's knights."

"Do you have another location in mind?"

Her soft voice in his ear shocked him. Damn, Meghan was going to be the death of him.

"Milady, you shouldn't talk so boldly to me. I have barely enough restraint as it is with regards to you."

"I cannot talk plainly to the man I love?"

Every hair on Ethan's body stood on end at her words. Leaning back, he stared into her amazing eyes.

"What did you just say?"

Meghan opened her mouth as if to say more, but at that moment, a magical portal suddenly opened in the courtyard, the aperture facing the dirt and hovering a few feet in mid-air. Shouts from the Wolverines below could be heard as a harsh wind blasted through the doorway, stirring up a large cloud of dust.

"What the hell?" Ethan said, grasping Meghan's hand and leading her to the nearest set of stairs.

Without warning, something round and small fell through the portal and bounced on the ground with an ethereal ping. Only a moment later, both Rowan and Malnan fell through as well, hitting the ground hard. A massive plume of flame followed them only to skirt around a magical shield Malnan swiftly raised, covering them right before the portal closed.

An eerie silence descended upon the courtyard. Wolverines glanced nervously at each other in fear while Rowan gasped for breath, coughing in the dirt and clutching the Emerald of Estriel to his chest.

Malnan's chest heaved a few times as she, too, struggled to breathe before finally curling into a ball on the ground. Her deep, heart-wrenching sobs echoed throughout the courtyard.

"No! *Mynos!*" she screamed.

Chapter Fifteen

Ethan sprinted to where Malnan and Rowan lay, skidding on his knees in the dirt. "Malnan?" he yelled as he shook her shoulder. "What has happened? Are you all right?"

Rowan let out a choked sob as he rolled over and stared at Ethan with large, round eyes. "Ethan, get the king!"

Ethan moved as if to stand, but Malnan reached up and clutched his tunic, pulling him back down to the dirt. "Where is it?" she demanded.

"Where is what, Malnan?"

The green dragon looked around frantically, her slitted eyes taking in the courtyard. "The Crystal! It fell through just before us. No one is to touch it!" she called out. "Only a woman can wield it and live."

"But what of Mynos?" Ethan asked.

"Mynos is no longer bonded to it." A look of pain crossed Malnan's face. "Ethan, you must find the Crystal. Find it and—"

Whatever she planned to say was suddenly lost as a piercing shriek filled the air behind him. Every nerve-ending prickled on Ethan's skin. He jumped up from the ground, pulling his sword from its sheath.

"What is happening?" he demanded from no one in particular.

At that moment, both Malnan and Rowan hit the dirt, as if knocked back by some unseen force. Whirling about, Ethan scanned the yard and spied Meghan lying on the ground, unmoving.

"She touched it!" someone yelled.

"She picked it up," another one shouted.

"Meghan!" Ethan raced to her side, dropping his sword as he once again fell to his knees. "Meghan, sweetheart, can you hear me?"

Her skin was deathly pale, coated with a sheen of sweat. Meghan's body was limp as Ethan lifted her from the ground, lifeless in his arms.

"No! Oh, God, Meghan, answer me," he cried.

He shook her, desperately wondering what had happened. But glancing down her limp form, he saw for himself. Clutched in her left hand was the Crystal of Mynos.

"Oh God," Ethan whispered under his breath. "Oh my God."

"Ethan, who touched it?" Malnan demanded behind him, finally standing from the dirt. "The shock wave... We felt the shock wave!"

Ethan couldn't answer her. Rocking back and forth with Meghan in his arms, he could do no more than cry.

Malnan ran to him and gasped. "Ethan." She placed a hand on his shoulder. "Sir Ethan."

With red-rimmed eyes, he gazed at her. "Please tell me she's not dead. Please tell me she'll be all right!"

"The Crystal has bonded to her. But she has no magical ability to buffer its effect. Her mind has cracked, Sir Ethan."

"What does that mean?" he asked, fear gripping his heart.

"It means the power of the Crystal will slowly kill her. She

111

will not awaken."

Ethan's stomach bottomed out from under him. "She's dying?" he whispered. "No, I will *not* accept that. Not her. Not my Meghan."

He felt as if he was going to be sick. Meghan had just professed her love for him not more than a few minutes ago, and now he was losing her? He couldn't lose her. Not now. Not ever.

"Can't we break the bond?" he asked, a shred of hope in his eyes. "Arianna was once released from the bond."

"Arianna was released by Mynos, my son. I'm afraid he is the only one capable of breaking the bond of his Crystal."

"Where is Mynos?" Sir Sebastian asked as he ran over to them, glancing around the courtyard.

"I must tell the king of what has happened," Malnan said absently as she turned to look at the Captain of the Guard.

"I have already sent Briand to fetch Geoffrey. Is there anything we can do for Meghan?" he said.

Ethan still held her in his arms, smoothing her hair and kissing her cool brow.

Malnan bit her lip with worry. "There might be a way."

"What? What is it?" Ethan demanded.

"If Meghan was enchanted with magic, that might give her the buffer she needs to fight the bonding."

"Anything, Malnan, please just save her!" Ethan was beyond caring how pathetic he was.

"The most powerful enchantment I know is..."

"What?"

"The Remembrance." Malnan held his gaze for a few agonizing moments. "She needs someone to be enchanted to."

"I'll do it," Ethan said, without hesitation.

"Consider first, before you decide, Sir Ethan," Malnan told him in concern. "This spell will be permanent, as only the one who casts the spell can safely remove it. As long as she is bonded to the Crystal, she must be enchanted with the Remembrance, and I do not know when her bonding can be...severed."

"I have made my decision, Malnan," Ethan said stoically. "I love her. I cannot lose her."

The dragon looked at him for a moment and nodded, kneeling in the dirt beside him. "I must warn you of this before I enchant you. Most people, when enchanted with the Remembrance, are children and do not remember. However there are a few who are enchanted as adults. It will be hard for you to adjust to it at first. Her thoughts will be yours, you will be able to find her at will, and you can silently speak to her. You will know her memories and see her life flash before you. Her mind will be ever-present in yours."

"I am not afraid of it."

"It will overwhelm you at first, but the images, scents, and sounds will fade after awhile. You will be able to recall them whenever you wish. But never, *ever* break the enchantment without me. Is that understood?"

Ethan nodded. "Yes."

Reaching out her hands, Malnan placed one hand on his head and one on Meghan's.

"Close your eyes, Sir Ethan," the dragon said gently. "This might hurt."

Chapter Sixteen

Ethan screamed as shards of fire exploded behind his eyes. His head whirled and he felt as if a sword had pierced his skull. Unfamiliar events played out in his mind—flashes of Meghan's life as a child, he assumed. A sunny day at a quiet creek, cleaning the fireplace, hanging the laundry.

An oppressive weight settled on his chest. It was hard to draw breath, but he continued to kneel on the ground, clutching onto Meghan's hand. His entire body trembled and his stomach lurched. He wouldn't be able to endure much more of this without getting sick.

Suddenly, it was over, and he fell onto the dirt, gasping. His skin was covered with sweat, and all he could do was moan.

"Are you all right, Sir Ethan?"

The concerned voice of Malnan hovered somewhere above him, but he couldn't answer. All he could concentrate on was the other strange presence in his head. Someone touched him— a hand pressed into his back and a warmth spread throughout his body. His breathing became easier and the nausea passed. But the presence in his mind remained.

"Do you feel her?" Malnan asked.

"I think so," he panted, attempting to push himself from the ground. "I no longer feel...alone."

At that moment, Meghan groaned, her eyes fluttering. "Meghan?" Ethan crawled to her, cradling her head in his lap. "Can you hear me?"

Despite Malnan's magic which eased some of his pain, he still felt a deep ache. Malnan answered his unspoken question.

"You are feeling her discomfort, Sir Ethan. Through your new bond. Try thinking to her. She might hear you."

Ethan swallowed hard. He felt Meghan's pain? *A lot more than thoughts must be exchanged through the Remembrance bond.*

"Meghan? Do you hear me?"

She tossed her head from side to side. "Sir Ethan?"

His eyes flew to the dragon. "She heard me!"

"Try again. She needs you now more than ever."

"Meghan, can you open your eyes for me?"

A few agonizing moments passed before her eyes fluttered open. They were ringed with tears. "Sir Ethan, I knew it was you." Her words melted his heart. "What happened?"

"You touched the Crystal of Mynos, milady. Not a very smart thing to do, if you ask me. You have everyone in the courtyard worried sick."

Meghan gave him an exhausted smile. "I am sorry. But Malnan dropped it. I did not know I shouldn't touch it."

"Don't worry yourself," Ethan said mentally, stroking her hair. *"You'll be weak for a while, but you should be all right."*

"Your mouth isn't moving. How can you talk if your mouth doesn't move?"

He gave her a grin. *"In order to protect you from the Crystal's magic, Malnan had to enchant you and me with the Remembrance. We can think to each other now and hear each other's thoughts."*

"You mean... *Can you hear me?*"

Nodding, he watched as understanding crossed her face. "I don't believe it."

"Believe it, Daughter," Malnan said gravely. "It was Sir Ethan who saved your life. He is the buffer you need to shield you from the Crystal's power. And until we can have Mynos break its hold on you, I'm afraid you'll have to stay bound to your young Wolverine."

"I cannot argue with a dragon," she sighed.

Ethan smiled.

"Here, let me take that." Malnan leaned over and took the Crystal, lifting it gingerly from Meghan's hands. "You do not need to carry such a burden, Daughter. You are already bonded to it. Holding it in your hand would merely prolong your fatigue."

"Thank you," she said, glancing back at Ethan. "I'm so tired. Will you take me back to my room?"

Ethan stood, sweeping Meghan into his arms. *"It would be my pleasure,"* he whispered in her mind, still amazed that he could.

He knew she was confused and frightened, but she hid it well. Her weariness was seeping into his own energy, making him tired also. He couldn't help but yawn.

Just as he crossed the courtyard toward the castle, King Geoffrey sprinted past with Briand in tow, apparently intent on intercepting Malnan. It was just as well. Ethan longed to lie next to Meghan and sleep the day away. After what she'd just endured, she deserved to rest, and he'd be damned if he wouldn't stay with her, not after what she'd confessed to him on the battlements.

She was in love with him. For now, that was all that

mattered.

CB

Geoffrey stood in front of Malnan and Rowan, both of whom looked as if they'd been through a hellish battle. Their clothing was dirty, as was their skin, and Malnan's cheeks were marred with the trails of tears. Each of them seemed in shock.

"What has happened?" he demanded. He'd only heard the hasty, terrified summons of Sir Briand of Breckenwood, one of his youngest Wolverines, that Malnan had returned. But all was not well. Dark thoughts raced through Geoffrey's mind at what could have happened. When Arianna had screamed mentally that she'd felt a magical shock wave, he could only guess.

Malnan wiped her face before answering. "It is better if I tell you in private, Your Majesty." Without wasting another second, she gestured to Rowan who held the Emerald of Estriel in his hand. A magical portal ripped open, leading to Mynos's lair. Geoffrey cocked a brow, but didn't question the dragon as he stepped through. Once Malnan and Rowan had followed him, the doorway consumed itself until it was gone.

Geoffrey didn't mince his words once he was on the other side. "Arianna felt a magical shock wave. What is going on?"

Rowan nodded, his face grave. "Sir Duncan's sister touched the Crystal of Mynos."

Geoffrey's jaw dropped as he took that in. "My God. Is she all right?"

"For now," Malnan said, running her hand through her mass of green hair. "But that's not the worst of our news."

Glancing around, Geoffrey finally realized Mynos wasn't with them. "Where's Mynos?"

Malnan and Rowan glanced at each other. "He's...he's..." Malnan couldn't go on. Rowan placed a hand on her shoulder, gazing at the king.

"Your Majesty, Mynos touched the Dragon's Flame. He...wasn't able to shield himself from the curse of the gem."

Every inch of Geoffrey's skin prickled. "What are you saying, Rowan?"

"I'm saying Mynos is...he's—"

"Cursed," Malnan finished. "Mynos is cursed."

"*What?*" Geoffrey could hardly believe his ears.

"We couldn't do anything," Rowan continued. "It was almost instantaneous. King Kaas opened the portal to the cave where the Flame rested, and we found it easily enough. It was held in the hand of a skeleton, presumably the very same man who'd braved the madness as the rhyme led us to believe. Once we'd stepped through the magical doorway, it filled the cavern with a beautiful red glow. When we got closer, it knew Mynos and Malnan, and even called them by name."

"It was almost as if Djendorl was pleased to see us," Malnan said. "The gem called out to me, and to Mynos as well. I began to walk forward, but Mynos held me back and lifted the Crystal, ready to lash out with his magic and destroy it, but he hesitated."

Rowan cleared his throat, still visibly shaken as he wrung his hands in front of him. "The Dragon's Flame is more powerful than we ever gave it credit for, Geoffrey. It was able to pierce even Mynos's resolve. I tried to shake him out of it, but he flung me across the cavern with his magic. Before either Malnan or I knew what he intended, he'd lunged for the Flame."

Tears collected in Malnan's eyes. "The moment he touched it, his bond with the Crystal was severed, and he screamed with an intensity that shook the very foundation of the cavern. I
118

knew in that moment Mynos couldn't let go. He couldn't fight it. His skin became red and he turned his sights on us. But it wasn't him. It wasn't Mynos!"

"The only thing I could think to do was make a portal back to the castle," Rowan said. "We were too shocked to do much more than stare in disbelief, and by the time I knew we had to do something, Mynos began..."

"What? Tell me!" Geoffrey tried hard to hold his emotions in check, but it was nearly impossible as his entire body shook from head to toe.

"He began to beat us back with his fire. Even in his human form, he can breathe flames. Our only option was to retreat. That's when we fell through the portal in the courtyard. Since Mynos was no longer bonded to his Crystal, it would have bonded to the first person to pick it up."

"Meghan." The king heaved a sigh, knowing all too well what the bonding of the Crystal might do to her. His own wife, Queen Arianna, had been bonded to the talisman as well.

Rowan nodded gravely.

Malnan wiped her eyes. "I had to enchant Meghan with the Remembrance as a buffer for the Crystal's magical energy, but I'm afraid that's not going to keep its power at bay for long."

"Who did you enchant her to?"

"Sir Ethan, Your Majesty."

Geoffrey nodded absently before throwing up his hands. "What the *hell* are we going to do?"

All three of them stared at each other in grim silence.

Cʒ

A dark cloud descended upon the castle as Sebastian

prepared his men for battle. His orders came from King Geoffrey himself, who'd told him to prepare for anything.

Word spread quickly, and already his men were whispering about Mynos being cursed by the Dragon's Flame. Most of the Wolverines were stoic, going through the motions of preparing Castle Templestone for a siege. But Sebastian knew better. His men were terrified of fighting Mynos, they merely hid their fear behind the bravado of their training.

Most of them could remember how Mynos had single-handedly decimated Queen Darragh's army a few years before. They knew they were no match for a dragon bent on destruction. Even Sebastian felt fear trickle down his spine.

But they had King Kaas and his Army of Magi at their back, as well as Mynos's own Crystal. Sebastian hoped Meghan could somehow figure out a way to channel its magic. If she couldn't, they were all in for one hell of a fight.

Chapter Seventeen

"I can feel it."

Meghan's voice inside Ethan's head startled him. He'd brought Meghan to her chambers, only to lie down beside her, sheltering her with his body. He had the uncanny urge to keep his skin in contact with hers, and when it wasn't, he felt a strange sense of loss. He had no idea if that was part of the Remembrance, but he was content to stay right where he was.

"Feel what?" he asked aloud, absently running his fingers through her hair.

"The Crystal." Meghan turned toward his chest. "I can feel it tugging on me. It...wants to be held, to be wielded."

"But you cannot wield it. You have no magical ability." She shivered at his words and he pulled her closer.

"I know. It's almost as if it wants me to try."

"That Crystal would do nothing more than suck the life out of you."

A long silence followed his words until Meghan spoke once again in his mind. *"I'm sorry I touched it. I'm so sorry, Sir Ethan."*

He heaved a sigh. "You didn't know, Meghan. I'm not mad at you."

She sniffled, wiping at her eyes when her body stiffened. *"Oh no."*

Ethan rose up on one of his elbows to look down on her. "What's the matter?"

She looked at him with shock. Her fear radiated through their bond and Ethan's heart began to race. "What is it?"

"The Crystal... It's telling me about Mynos, he...he..."

She didn't have to say another word. Ethan knew her thoughts. *"Cursed? How is that possible?"*

"He touched the Dragon's Flame. He thought he could conquer the madness. Oh God, it's not him anymore!"

Ethan tried to make sense of her words. "Then...who is he?"

Meghan trembled and took his hand, twining her fingers with his. *"Djendorl."*

⑃

Mynos was screaming. Again and again, he tried to conjure his magic, but to no avail. No matter how hard he tried, his body would no longer respond to his commands. He was helpless, looking out through his own eyes. All he could do was watch as the spirit of the evil red dragon within the Dragon's Flame took hold of his body.

"Ah, Mynos," he heard his own voice say. "I never thought it would be you who would finally find me buried in the Mountains of the Night. Is it not a cruel irony to become the very one I detested millennia ago? I cannot believe my luck."

"You are going to pay for this, Djendorl. Most dearly. I will not sit idly by and let you do this."

"Oh, but you will, *Your Majesty.* You have no other choice."

Mynos felt the familiar weaves of magic pulsing through his limbs as Djendorl tapped into his power and channeled a force upward, making the entire cave rumble all around them. Clumps of rocks and dirt fell from high above, and bright sunlight poured into the cavern as a giant hole blasted its way through the bedrock.

"Blessed freedom!" Djendorl shouted a split second before he began to shift Mynos's body into his draconic form. "To the skies we shall go, Mynos, you and I, scorching Lyndaria from the Mountains of the Night to the Silver Sea. What a beautiful world we'll create, my *king*. Built on the wails of women and children!"

Mynos fought as hard as he could, but Djendorl had a firm grip on his mind. The Dragon's Flame burned in Mynos's talons, but he could not let go of it. He damned himself for touching the gem, for thinking his strong magics would protect him. Now, his shining golden scales were gone, replaced by burnished red ones, glistening in the dazzling sun.

Djendorl shot through the hole at the top of the cave and into the skies beyond, laughing hideously at Mynos's attempts to reclaim his body.

"Give up, Mynos," the red dragon shouted against the wind. "It is futile. You can do nothing to stop me!"

Mynos screamed once more—but no one heard him.

◌ℬ

Arianna bit her bottom lip so hard, she winced. She tried her hardest not to cry, but it was nearly impossible as she watched her husband pace in front of the windows of his study. His emotions were in turmoil. She could feel them as clearly as she felt her own.

Malnan had refused to sit as well, despite being told to rest. Arianna could only imagine what she must be going through. She'd lived for millennia trapped inside her Jewel, only to find her mate and lose him once more to a powerful curse.

King Kaas sat next to Rowan, both of whom seemed speechless. Kaas had folded his hands on his lap while Rowan looked as if he needed a good night's sleep.

"It's been a few hours," Geoffrey said, breaking the silence. "Mynos hasn't attempted to attack the castle."

"It's not Mynos," Malnan replied.

Arianna was confused. "What do you mean?"

"It's not Mynos, Daughter. I've been trying to contact him magically ever since he touched the Flame, and he hasn't answered. He either can't answer or he won't. That creature who attacked us in the cave was not my mate. It was Djendorl."

The hair on the back of Arianna's neck stood on end. "Djendorl...has possessed Mynos?"

Malnan looked tortured as she gazed at her. "I believe so."

"But how is that possible?" Geoffrey asked, throwing up his hands. "I thought Mynos was a formidable magic user. How could he succumb so easily?"

"Mynos might have indeed been king of the dragons, Your Majesty, but he was in no way the strongest. The older the dragon, the more powerful they become, learning new and better ways to cast their magic. Djendorl was one of the oldest dragons I can remember."

"How do we stop him?" The voice of Kaas rang throughout the study. "Perhaps the question I should ask is *can* we stop him?"

Silence followed his words.

"What about his Crystal? Surely we can find a way to use

it." Arianna looked at everyone.

"Not with Meghan bound to it, Daughter," Malnan told her. "She does not have the power to wield it. If she tried, the Crystal would kill her, regardless of the Remembrance."

"Besides," Rowan began, "it would do us no good. The Crystal cannot harm Mynos. I do not believe the Crystal's enchantment would differentiate between Djendorl or Mynos if they are both in the same body."

"Are they in the same body?" Kaas asked, turning his eyes to Rowan. "Perhaps Mynos's soul is now trapped within the Dragon's Flame."

"I do not believe that is how the curse works." Malnan sighed, finally taking a seat. "It is my understanding that Djendorl's soul overcomes your own, making you a prisoner in your own body."

Arianna gasped. "You mean Mynos can see what he's doing?"

The dragon nodded. "I believe so. And he cannot do a thing to stop it."

"Mynos is a trusted friend," Geoffrey said with a sigh, running a hand through his hair. "I do not want to kill him if we don't have to. We *must* find a way to break this curse."

Malnan's eyes widened, but she said nothing. Arianna shivered. Would they have to kill Mynos in order to save Lyndaria? She prayed her husband never had to make that decision.

Chapter Eighteen

Meghan snuggled into Ethan's warmth, but he wasn't sleeping. He was thinking, about her, about Mynos, about the Remembrance. It was odd, hearing random snippets of his thoughts, but it was comforting as well, knowing he was closer to her than anyone else had ever been.

It hadn't been that long ago Meghan had wished for a love not unlike the romance between the king and queen. Now she was magically enchanted—just as they—to a most wonderful man.

Ethan scoffed, apparently hearing her thoughts. "You don't know me that well if you think I'm wonderful." His fingers trailed through her hair, making her sigh at the sensation. She couldn't help but smile.

"And you don't think very highly of yourself if you do not. You are more amazing than you give yourself credit for."

"Do you truly love me?"

His unexpected query made Meghan's heart skip a beat. She blushed from head to toe, remembering the words she'd said to him on the battlements.

"I never expected to feel something so strong so soon, Sir Ethan," she whispered, stroking his face. "But yes, I do love you."

His eyes searched hers for a few moments and no matter how hard she tried, she couldn't read his mind.

"Then perhaps the time has come that you shouldn't be so formal, milady. Just call me Ethan."

"All right. *Ethan.*" His smile brightened up the room and Meghan's breath caught. He was beautiful.

"No, milady, you are mistaken," he said, his eyes twinkling. "*You* are the beautiful one."

He brought his lips to hers, kissing her lightly. His mouth was warm, moving gently, demanding nothing. Meghan caressed the back of his neck, just barely weaving her fingers in his hair. His entire body responded and he rolled on top of her, his tongue asking entrance into her mouth.

Meghan knew what he wanted. Ethan wanted to make love to her more than anything in the world, she could feel it. His need fueled her own, making her grasp his head so he could not get away.

"Meghan..." His voice in her head startled her, but she answered regardless.

"What?"

"I want you." His real voice was loud in comparison to his thoughts.

"I know." She swiped her thumb across his cheek.

"Now is not a good time for this."

"When will it ever be?"

"I don't know." He broke eye contact by resting his head on her shoulder.

"Ethan," she breathed into his ear, making him shudder. "I'm bonded to Mynos's Crystal and he himself has been cursed by the Dragon's Flame. I'm terrified of what is to become of me. Until Mynos's curse is broken, I will be bonded to his talisman.

It is altogether possible King Geoffrey might send you on another mission to God knows where. This may be all the time we have together."

Ethan leaned back, gazing deeply into her eyes. "My sword has been calling me to arms for the past hour now," he said, his voice low. "Sebastian has apparently ordered the castle to be prepared for battle. I must see to my duties."

Meghan nodded slowly and swallowed hard. "I understand." She tried her hardest not to let her disappointment seep through their bond, but Ethan's look of anguished surrender told her she hadn't been successful.

With a groan, he returned his mouth to hers. *"Damn it, let them wait."*

Instantly, Meghan's body was on fire, burning with the need to feel his touch upon her skin. Her fervor shocked Ethan but he didn't question it. Firefury had indeed been calling him to the battlements for quite some time. But he couldn't bear to leave her. She was frightened, that much he knew. And her words rang true. In light of all that had happened this could indeed be their only time together for a while.

He didn't care about anything beyond the woman in his arms. All he wanted was to possess her, make her his in truth. With skilled hands, he bunched her dress to her thighs and she deftly opened her legs for him. His heart raced when her hands slipped underneath his tunic, caressing the skin of his chest.

"You're getting ahead of me." He grinned, lowering his head to plant kisses on her neck.

"We have no time to make love at our leisure, milord."

Her words amused him and he chuckled. "Indeed. Perhaps we should hurry things along?"

"You read my thoughts." With one swift tug, Meghan had tossed Ethan's tunic across the room.

128

"Exactly who's doing the seducing, my dear?" he exclaimed, frantically ripping at the buttons of her gown.

"Ah, Ethan, you do not need to seduce me. I am most willing." Meghan shoved his shoulders back and he lost his balance above her, falling to the bed with a thud. Before he'd realized what she'd done, she crawled over him, a playful grin on her face.

"Good God, woman, are you *sure* you're a virgin?"

She arched her brow at him in a most bewitching way. "You'll find out soon enough, won't you?"

Ethan would have laughed out loud, but Meghan's mouth on his stopped him. For long, tender moments, he couldn't come up for air as she held his face in her hands, kissing him with an innocence he'd never experienced before. He knew by the way she pressed against him she hadn't been kissed by many men, a fact he was most happy about. The women he'd been with in years past hadn't been so pure. He didn't care then.

But he cared now.

Something about this woman made him want to lose himself within her, breathe her in and never let her go. Perhaps it was the Remembrance, but he doubted it. He'd wanted her well before they were enchanted by the spell. She was Duncan's sister and that seemed fitting somehow, as if Duncan knew she'd be the perfect woman for him, even from beyond the grave.

Once Meghan's buttons were undone, he yanked the fabric off her shoulders and leaned up to taste her exposed skin. She gasped and every inch of him screamed to touch her. He couldn't pull off her dress fast enough.

"Impatient?" she asked with a grin. Her hands flew all over him, igniting his blood. He smiled wickedly when her breasts were finally exposed, bouncing slightly.

"You have no idea."

Ethan pushed her back only to lean over her once more, his mouth latching onto her nipple. She tasted like honeysuckle as his tongue swirled upon her, stiffening her peak. Meghan cried out, but it wasn't in pain. Her voice in his head whispered his name over and over while she writhed beneath him, apparently just as desperate to feel his skin against hers. With one more tug, her dress was gone and he didn't waste any time tearing at her drawers.

Ethan latched on to her other breast, delighting in the whimpers she gave him. Time seemed to stop as he brought his lips back up to hers. Meghan's hand searched for the ties of his breeches between them, and he lifted himself above her without breaking their kiss. Once the ties were loosened, she slipped her hands inside, making him groan in pleasure-pain. Their eyes locked when her hands timidly touched his hardened length. There was no need for words. Despite her fear of his size, she wanted to continue.

"You're sure?" he asked mentally.

Meghan nodded, still fondling him, driving him wild.

Ethan kicked off his breeches and finally worked her drawers from around her ankles. He nudged his knee between her legs and she opened without hesitation.

"Make love to me, Ethan," she panted, her eyes dark with desire.

"Your first time will be uncomfortable," he told her, running his hands over the soft flesh of her belly. Lower and lower he went, until his fingers circled upon her wet skin. She rewarded him with a shuddering gasp, her mouth open and inviting. He couldn't help but lean into her lips, thrusting his tongue and continuing his erotic caress.

Meghan wrapped her leg around his hips, joining him in his passion. "Don't make me beg."

"Never, milady," he breathed, bringing himself flush with her body. "I just want to make sure you're prepared."

"I'm more than ready."

His entry was slow and steady. She mewled low in her throat and pulled him closer, but never once told him to stop his advance. She was tight and wet, and Ethan groaned at the sheer willpower it took for him not to drive deeply into her.

Meghan tilted her hips, asking for more. With a few gentle thrusts, he was completely sheathed, reveling in the feeling of her warmth surrounding him. He loved this woman. There would be no turning back now.

"You *love* me?" She'd heard his thoughts. Gazing into her shimmering eyes, he saw her amazement. Her fingers stroked his cheek.

He blushed, but could not deny it. The Remembrance seemed to strengthen his own feelings that were already there. He was more than in love with Meghan. He was *madly* in love with her. All he could do was nod before he kissed her once more, pulling out of her warmth only to push forward again and again. Her kisses became deeper, more passionate, and he knew she was telling him that she loved him without words.

Stroke for stroke she matched his rhythm, keeping time with his pounding heart. Before he knew it, they were both caught up in a maelstrom of sensation, crying out their pleasure through their tears of joy.

Chapter Nineteen

Djendorl rejoiced in his new-found freedom. For far too long he'd been buried inside the Mountains of the Night, with no means of escape. Having Mynos himself find him was beyond good fortune—it was destiny. For eons, he'd dreamt of humbling the mighty golden dragon, "His Majesty", Mynos the Wise. He'd had the audacity to demand respect and undying loyalty so long ago. Djendorl would have rebelled, of course, but the knowledge that Lyndaria's king held the Crystal of Mynos had stopped him.

Djendorl was no coward. But he'd been a pawn in his king's agenda on more than one occasion, and there was no forgiveness for the way Mynos had used him in the past. He'd only obeyed Mynos's orders for the sake of his mate, Biyanti, who'd thought the sun rose and set in her king. She'd been a neutral white dragon, uncaring if Djendorl burned the countryside with his magical fire. But she believed in the chain of command, and recognized the golden dragon as her monarch.

After Biyanti's brutal death at the hands of a few fanatic citizens of Lyndaria, Djendorl had plotted against Mynos in secret. The people who'd killed his beautiful mate did so in order to get to *him*—Djendorl knew how their puny minds worked. It was revenge for burning their villages and killing their families.

But Mynos had done nothing. He stood by and did *nothing*, claiming Djendorl had brought the tragedy upon himself. Mynos had not retaliated against the peoples of his ally, King Timothy, ruler of the Four Realms, regardless of the fact that they'd killed a fellow dragon, one of Mynos's own subjects.

That knowledge had festered within Djendorl's heart, and more than anything he'd wanted to lash out, take Mynos's golden flesh between his talons and feast on his warm, gushing blood. But Iruindyll had had a different plan. She knew Djendorl hated Mynos with his very soul. She'd convinced him to wait for his revenge, that she had a plan to kill *Mynos's* mate, bringing him agony such as he'd never known.

Her plan to steal the Crystal millennia ago had been a sound one. Mynos had rallied all his subjects, just as Iruindyll had predicted, and Djendorl had joined him in the fight, as every other loyal dragon. However, he was far from loyal.

The destruction Iruindyll's army created had been a beautiful sight to behold—fire had scorched the ground and the smell of burning flesh had filled the air. Djendorl's heart raced at the mere memory. It had been Heaven.

But the moment he'd faked his own death, falling to the earth in a spectacular display of lightning and flame, Mynos's mate had found him, thinking he was truly dead. Djendorl hadn't had time to react before Malnan's magic consecrated his body, hardening it into a red gem. He'd screamed and tried his hardest to escape, but it was useless. His soul was trapped. The only consolation he'd had was the knowledge that Malnan had died on the battlefield that day. That was one of the last things he could remember before his consciousness faded—until an elf found his gem some years later.

But when Mynos had come to the cave where Djendorl had been buried after wreaking glorious havoc on the elven kingdom, Malnan had been with him. Djendorl had no idea how she'd come back to life, but he was determined she wouldn't live long.

"Don't you dare do anything to Malnan."

"Why, Mynos," Djendorl said, chuckling. "I thought you'd fallen asleep after I destroyed that vast forest not too long ago."

"If you touch her, Djendorl, I'll make sure your pain is a thousand-fold."

The cool evening air breezed by Djendorl's draconic face and he smiled at Mynos's words. "You are in no position to make threats, my king. It is only fair you should live without Malnan, just as I must live without Biyanti."

"You know nothing," Mynos spat in his head. *"I have lived without Malnan for millennia!"*

"Yet she has come back to you. How *lucky* you are."

"You would be so quick to kill her? To destroy the only chance dragonkind has to rebuild its former glory?"

Djendorl pondered that thought for a moment. Perhaps he had been too hasty. Iruindyll's plan had worked a little too well. Maybe she'd always meant to wipe out her competition by killing every single dragon. If that were the truth, she would have betrayed *him* as surely as he'd betrayed Mynos on the battlefield.

"Iruindyll is dead," Mynos growled. *"You will gain no ally in her."*

"It is just as well," Djendorl sighed. "I would have killed her myself anyway." After a few moments of pondering Mynos's words, he began to laugh. "Oh, Your Majesty, this is perfect. Just perfect! Malnan is the last female of our kind, isn't she?"

Mynos's silence answered his question. Perhaps he wouldn't kill Malnan after all. Not if she could bear his offspring.

"No!" Mynos yelled.

"Oh yes," Djendorl whispered, flying low over the landscape. "Malnan will be mine and you can do *nothing.*"

Soaring over a foothill, he spotted a large city, nestled against a serene lake. If Djendorl wasn't mistaken, that was Krey Lake, just past the Mountains of the Night. At this time of the evening, everyone would be settling down to dinner or slipping into their beds after a long day of work.

Fires burned in his belly, demanding to be released. His mouth actually watered at the thought of leveling the city and fulfilling his appetite on the flesh of unsuspecting villagers.

"Djendorl, no. Please, I beg of you. Do what you want to me, but spare the City of Krey."

The red dragon didn't answer. Instead, he circled the city once before releasing his breath in a mighty heave, spewing magical flames down upon buildings, trees, and fleeing people. Within a matter of moments, the entire city burned, filling the dark sky with an orange glow as the screams of women and children rent the air.

"No!" Mynos screeched.

Djendorl grinned at the splendor of fiery chaos he'd created. He swooped low to satisfy his gnawing hunger.

ઝ

King Geoffrey stood on the battlements of Castle Templestone long after the sun had set. He scanned the skies himself, looking for a trace of Mynos or Djendorl—whoever was now inhabiting the dragon's body. Hours had passed since Malnan and Rowan had returned from their mission, and Geoffrey had been convinced Mynos would have attacked the castle shortly thereafter. But the dragon hadn't been spotted all day. Not knowing where he was made a knot form in Geoffrey's belly. If he wasn't here, then where was he?

Geoffrey felt helpless, unable to do anything, unable to come up with a solution to break the curse on Mynos. Kaas had told him the elven mages hundreds of years ago hadn't been successful in breaking the bond of the Flame when his own people had been cursed by it. How could they possibly fight a dragon who could easily decimate the entire countryside?

"You all right?" Sebastian's voice broke through his ponderings. His old friend leaned on the crenellation, gazing at the night sky.

"No." Geoffrey barely shook his head. "I'm king of Lyndaria and I have no idea what the hell to do. How can I lead this country if I cannot fight a threat such as this? Mynos is a *dragon*, Seb. He can kill us all without sparing us a thought."

"But we have Malnan."

Geoffrey sighed deeply. "She would not kill her mate, nor can she harm him. As I understand it, Malnan's magic isn't even close to Mynos's power."

"What about the Crystal?" Sebastian looked at him expectantly.

"It's bonded to Duncan's sister. We cannot use it without killing her. She has no magical ability."

"But she was just enchanted to Ethan with the Remembrance."

"That is true," Geoffrey said, also leaning against the crenellation. "But that was to give her a buffer against the magic of the talisman, the magic that is always emanating from
136

it. The Crystal's full power would kill her if she tried to wield that magic."

Sebastian whistled through his teeth. "And Mynos is the only one who can break that bond?"

"Yes."

A long silence descended upon them before Sebastian spoke again. "Do you think Kaas's Army of Magi can protect us?"

"I hope so," Geoffrey whispered. "For all our sakes."

"Your Majesty!"

Geoffrey turned to look over his shoulder only to see Kaas taking the steps to the battlements two at a time. The elven king was out of breath by the time he reached the top. "My scouts have sent word," he panted. "Mynos has been spotted."

Geoffrey's skin prickled and he swallowed hard in an effort to calm his thundering heart. "Where?"

Kaas placed his hand on Geoffrey's shoulder and squeezed. "The City of Krey, Your Majesty."

"That's on the border of the Dragon's Death Mountains."

Kaas nodded. "Sire, the city has been destroyed. Razed to the ground."

Geoffrey stumbled back. "Dear God! The people?"

"I do not know. But my scout reported mass casualties. And Mynos himself... His scales were red."

"It's not him. It's not Mynos." Geoffrey's voice cracked.

"Djendorl." That one word from Kaas fell between them like a stone.

"Then it has begun." Geoffrey swept past Kaas to the stairs. "Sebastian, summon Ethan."

"Of course, Sire."

Geoffrey raced down the steps, steeling his emotions. He couldn't afford to let his men see his unease, no matter how much hopelessness gnawed at his heart.

Chapter Twenty

Meghan's head spun as Ethan lay panting above her. He gave her a few soft kisses along her neck before bringing his mouth to hers.

"Did I hurt you?" He shifted his hips and she closed her eyes tightly, sucking in her breath, trying not to moan at the sensation. He was still deeply rooted, seeming to enjoy teasing her as he gave her a wicked smile.

"No, you did not," she said, capturing his lips once more. "It was glorious."

Ethan leaned on his elbows to look down on her. "Truly?"

"Truly."

"No one has called my lovemaking glorious before. But I suppose it is because this is your first time."

"Ah, so you think I called it *glorious* because I have not the experience to know otherwise?"

He gave her a skeptical look. "Obviously."

"Well then, I simply must have more experience before I say such a thing in the future."

Ethan nodded, wagging his eyebrows. "Exactly my thoughts."

"Do you believe Lord Galen of Evendria is available this evening?"

She'd shocked him. Meghan couldn't stop her peals of laughter at Ethan's look of consternation.

"Nay, milady," he said sourly. "You shall not grace the bed of any other man while you are yet enchanted to me."

"Why?" she teased. "Because you are jealous?"

Ethan scoffed. "Hardly! It's because I wouldn't get a moment's peace with all that moaning you do."

Meghan's eyes widened. "Oh!" She smacked his shoulder and dodged his mouth until he finally captured her head in his hands. She struggled a moment through her giggles, but realized he hadn't tried to kiss her. His eyes seemed to look into her soul.

"It was indeed glorious, sweet Meghan." Hearing his voice in her head made his words somehow more intimate.

Her heart skipped a beat a moment before their lips touched. Bantering with Ethan was most enjoyable. She loved his sense of humor and silently thanked Malnan for bonding them with the Remembrance. If the time ever came that she was released from the clutches of the Crystal of Mynos, she hoped in her heart of hearts Sir Ethan of Krey would choose to keep their bond intact.

A bright light suddenly shone throughout the room, making Meghan squint with watery eyes. It came from the floor and Ethan laid his head on her shoulder with a deep sigh.

"Damn," he whispered.

"What is it?"

"Firefury. Sebastian must be summoning me directly. I've been away from my post for far too long."

"Will you get in trouble?" Meghan suddenly felt guilty for having him stay with her instead of seeing to his duties.

"No. Seb knows what we've both gone through. He will not

be angry with me. However, I'm afraid I must take my leave. I cannot dally any longer."

He rolled off the bed, casually looking for his clothing strewn about the room. Meghan lay there and admired his physical beauty as he donned his breeches.

"Keep looking at me like that, my dear, and I might just risk life and limb to stay here with you instead of seeing what's gotten into Sebastian's scabbard."

Meghan smiled. "How did you know I was looking at you?"

He turned as he donned his tunic. "Now that we are enchanted to one another, your mind is an open book."

"Oh? What am I thinking now?"

Ethan's cheeks actually reddened as he stooped to swipe his sword off the floor. "Have you no shame, woman?"

"Not where you're concerned."

Once his weapon was strapped to his waist, Ethan sat on the edge of the bed to slip on his boots. He bent low and gave Meghan a scalding kiss, one that made her toes curl.

"Stay right where you are, sweeting," he purred. "When I get back, I plan on keeping you naked in this bed for a fortnight."

Now it was Meghan's turn to blush as he gave her a wink and strode out the door with a grand flourish. She giggled to herself and slid deeper into the covers, a wide grin on her face.

Cʒ

"Ethan, sit down."

With an arched brow, Ethan sat, watching his king as he paced the study. Geoffrey appeared to have aged a decade, as his face was lined with wrinkles and his hair uncombed. His bid for Ethan to sit was not a request, but a demand.

Sebastian sat next to Ethan who glanced at him with concern, while King Kaas, Rowan and Malnan all stood by King Geoffrey's massive mahogany desk.

Taking a deep breath, Geoffrey stopped pacing to gaze into Ethan's eyes. By the look on his face, Ethan knew it wouldn't be good news. His heart suddenly lodged in his throat.

"We have found Mynos," Geoffrey began, his eyes shimmering. "But I'm afraid it is not... Dear Lord, there is no easy way to say this."

"Say what, Your Majesty?" Ethan looked frantically around the room, taking in the solemn faces.

"The City of Krey no longer stands."

Silence descended upon everyone as Ethan tried to make sense of Geoffrey's words.

"I...I don't understand." Swallowing the lump in his throat, he tried his hardest not to shift in his seat. His heartbeat was deafening, and he feared his king's answer.

Geoffrey tossed a glance to Malnan, who seemed to have pity on the young monarch. "What the king is trying to say, Son, is that Djendorl has taken over my mate's body and...destroyed the City of Krey."

Ethan's eyes went wide and shock flooded through him as every inch of his skin prickled with fear and grief. Tears brimmed behind his eyes and he couldn't stop himself from shaking violently.

"My *family?*" It was hard to draw breath as his chest constricted. He feared the dragon's reply with everything inside of him.

"From the continuing reports of King Kaas's scouts, it would seem unlikely anyone survived. I am sorry, Sir Ethan."

He couldn't sit any longer. Shoving his fingers through his hair, he tried to maintain his composure as he roamed the study like a caged animal. But it was useless. Deep sobs ripped from his throat before he could stop them, and he sank to his knees.

Instantly Malnan was there, stroking his hair and cooing to him in a language he didn't understand. A warmth spread throughout his body and his breathing eased, but it didn't stop his cries of sorrow. His mother, father, aunts and uncles, and countless cousins—gone? He could barely take it all in.

"I need to go...to Krey, Your Majesty," he choked out. "I need to see for my-myself."

Geoffrey shook his head. "No, Ethan," he said gently. "Djendorl might still be in the area. I will send no envoy to Krey until I know the dragon has moved on. I cannot afford to lose good men."

"You've already lost good men!" He hadn't meant to shout his words, but shout them he did. Pushing Malnan's hands aside, Ethan stood once more, wiping his cheeks with the back of his hand. "How can I stand here and do nothing when my home has been annihilated?"

"You will not do 'nothing'." Geoffrey crossed the room to stand before him. "You will protect this castle—protect this country."

Ethan stared into Geoffrey's eyes, as hard as agates, telling him his king understood his pain but could not do a thing to ease it. He gave Geoffrey a sharp nod, his jaw set, regardless of the despair spiraling within him.

"We must use the Crystal." Kaas's soft voice seemed to float ethereally throughout the room. Ethan turned to glare at him.

"Don't you *dare* suggest we sacrifice Meghan's life."

"It is the only way, Sir Ethan."

143

"*No!*" Everyone in the room was taken aback. "The Crystal of Mynos will do *nothing* to save the dragon and well you know it. It cannot hurt him. Killing Meghan will not protect this country. I will not allow it!" Ethan was seething, his emotions raging out of control. He didn't care in the least if he offended two kings—he was not about to let these men decide the fate of the woman he loved.

"We cannot hurt Djendorl, not while he's in Mynos's body," Malnan said, placing a hand on Ethan's shoulder. "But we *can* destroy the Flame. If we destroy the vessel that houses Djendorl's soul, he will fade away into the afterlife."

Ethan turned his gaze to her. Malnan's strange, slitted eyes glimmered with concern. "You are a dragon," he said flippantly. "Why can't *you* destroy the talisman you yourself created?" He knew he'd hurt her, but he was well beyond caring.

Malnan gasped just as Geoffrey's face darkened. "You *will* be civil to Mynos's mate, Sir Ethan."

The green dragon held up her hand. "Please, Geoffrey, he asked a valid question." She turned her ancient eyes upon him, and for the first time, Ethan squirmed under their scrutiny. "I can create a magical talisman, but I cannot destroy one. My power is simply not that strong. Once a dragon's body is consecrated, the gem they create is pure magic, comparable to the magic the dragon was able to wield in life.

"Djendorl was very powerful, my son. Even though I created the Dragon's Flame, I cannot destroy it. I do not believe even Mynos himself could do so without the help of his Crystal."

Ethan took a moment before he responded, drawing in a deep breath. "The Crystal will kill Meghan if she tries to use it. She has no magical ability!"

"We know," Rowan said with a deep sigh. "But that might be a risk we'll have to take."

Ethan couldn't believe his ears. He felt as if he'd been punched in the gut as he glanced around the room, only to be met with silent stares.

"You are asking me to risk Meghan's life to save Mynos?"

"We are asking you to risk Meghan's life to save Lyndaria," Geoffrey said stoically. "If Djendorl destroys another of my cities, Ethan, I will not ask you again."

Ethan raged at Geoffrey's words, but knew somewhere in the back of his mind that if Djendorl was capable of leveling the City of Krey, he could easily wreak such havoc as Lyndaria had never known. He needed to be stopped—by any means possible.

"There has to be another way." He sounded pathetic. He knew his tears fell in torrents, but he couldn't hold them back, no matter how hard he tried.

"There is not," Kaas said with sympathy in his eyes. "We have a plan, but the amount of magic Meghan would have to wield would probably kill her."

As much as it pained his heart, Ethan looked at the elven king and asked him to continue.

"Thousands of years ago, the Crystal of Mynos was stolen from Castle Templestone by Sir Vincent of Westchester at the urgings of Iruindyll the dragon."

"The original war for the Crystal?" Ethan asked.

"Yes. The very war that killed dragonkind. Iruindyll had somehow learned that by linking her magic users and channeling their power through the talisman as one, her army would be nearly indestructible. This was how they succeeded in shielding themselves from the dragons' magic, as well as dropping them from the sky."

"What does this have to do with Meghan?" Ethan asked, confused.

Kaas gave him a half-grin. "I have the Army of Magi at my disposal. Every single elf in my service is a magic user in his own right, and only an accomplished mage can gain entrance into my army. If we can repeat history, if we can link my mages to focus as one through the Crystal, we have a chance to lure Djendorl into the open and destroy the Dragon's Flame."

Ethan's eyes were gritty. He rubbed them and tried his hardest to make sense of Kaas's words, but it was almost impossible. He was exhausted. "I don't understand. Only Meghan is bonded through the Crystal. How can your mages wield its power?"

"You underestimate the power of the Remembrance." Malnan's voice next to him made Ethan jump. He'd forgotten she was there.

Kaas nodded. "Yes. That is where Meghan's fragile mind would collapse. You see, every member of my army would have to be magically bonded to her through the Remembrance. Only through that magical bridge could they manipulate the power of Mynos's gem."

Ethan stood stunned. "Is that how Iruindyll...?"

"Yes, we believe so, Sir Ethan," Malnan said. "There is no other way I know of that would allow another person to wield the Crystal's power."

"If the Remembrance is that powerful, then perhaps I can convince the Crystal to let Meghan's mind go!" Hope lit in Ethan's soul. But his heart fell when Rowan shook his head.

"That will not work."

"Why?"

"Only Mynos himself can break the bond of the talisman."

"How do you know that?" Ethan challenged. "How do you know there isn't another way?"

"Because I have tried," Malnan said. "Long ago, not long after Mynos created the Crystal, I tried to break its bond with Sanael, a young man, the first mortal to ever touch it. I did not succeed."

King Geoffrey heaved a sigh. "Ethan. I am sorry. But this is our greatest hope of defeating Djendorl. We cannot afford to take our chances."

Ethan didn't answer him. Instead, he strode to the study doors and ripped them open so hard, they rattled in their frame. Without looking back, he charged down the hall with his hand on the hilt of his sword. He'd kill that damned dragon before they laid one finger on Meghan of Marynville.

Chapter Twenty-One

Meghan sat up in bed. All was not right. Ethan's roiling emotions became her own, and her heartbeat quickened with both fright and anger. He'd been summoned not too long ago, but already, she felt his trepidation within her. What had happened?

She tried contacting him mentally, but either he wasn't answering or she hadn't properly made contact with him. She bit her lip in worry, taking deep breaths in an effort to calm herself. Meghan rubbed her sweaty palms on the quilt that covered her and wondered if she should get dressed to seek Ethan out.

But before she threw the covers back, her door opened and Ethan walked in, slamming the door behind him. He didn't say one word to her—he didn't have to. The look on his face told her that whatever he'd learned, it wasn't good news. Meghan shuddered when his eyes met hers, twin flames burning her to the core.

Ethan unstrapped his sword and tore out of his shirt, stripping bare before her within a matter of moments. With purposeful strides, he made his way to the bed, tossing back the blankets himself, covering her with his large body.

He'd been crying; his eyes were red and puffy. Meghan's heart broke for him as she caressed his cheek.

"They will have to kill me before they kill you." His words shocked her and she gasped, clutching his shoulders.

"What are you talking about?" she whispered, afraid of his response.

Ethan sniffled, then laid his forehead on hers. Meghan's own eyes misted as well. "King Geoffrey and the others, they want to use the Crystal of Mynos to defeat Djendorl. He's somehow possessed Mynos's body and...and..."

He couldn't go on as he closed his eyes and wept.

"Ethan?" Meghan ran her fingers through his hair, trying hard not to sob. He didn't say anything else, but the scenes that flashed before her eyes brought terror to her heart.

The City of Krey had been burned to the ground.

"Ethan," she repeated. "I'm *so* sorry."

Images of his family and friends bombarded her and she felt his grief as deeply as her own. "Good God," she choked out. "All those people!"

"The Crystal is the only way to defeat the dragon." His words floated down to her, as if through a fog. She shook her head in an effort to clear her mind.

"The Crystal?"

"Yes," he answered, giving her gentle pecks across her face. "They have a plan, to link you with Kaas's Army of Magi in order to destroy the Dragon's Flame."

Meghan's skin pebbled and a dark dread overcame her. "But I'll die if I use the Crystal."

Ethan's silent nod tied her stomach in knots. She stared at him in horror, the realization of what she had to do finally hitting her.

"Is this the only way?"

"Yes," he breathed.

"Will it...hurt?"

"Oh God, Meghan..."

Clutching his face, she licked her lips and said brokenly, "If this is what needs to be done to save the kingdom, then I will do it. My one life does not compare to the countless thousands who will perish if we do nothing."

"No," Ethan growled.

"It is for the greater good."

Ethan's features twisted with despair. "*No!* I *cannot* let you go, Meghan. Not now. Not ever!"

Whatever words she'd planned to say died on her lips when Ethan's mouth captured hers with a desperate hunger. His tongue plunged again and again, making her whimper at his ardor, but she demanded more of him. Her legs wrapped around his hips of their own accord, and before she had time to think, he was inside her, touching her deeply within.

"*I love you, woman,*" his voice whispered in her mind. "*I just found you. I cannot allow you to sacrifice yourself. You must understand.*"

"*I do understand,*" she answered. "*But that doesn't change what needs to be done.*"

"*I can't do it, Meghan. I can't watch you die!*"

Meghan's heart skipped a beat at his tortured words. Despite Ethan's feelings of helplessness, she knew this had to be done. No more words were said as they concentrated on each other, and Meghan lost herself in Ethan's possession, giving her heart fully to him and only him—the man of her dreams.

ᘓ

Ethan lay awake long into the night. He stared at the

ceiling while Meghan slept, her soft breaths caressing the skin of his chest. If he concentrated hard enough, he knew what she was dreaming about—being back in Marynville with Duncan.

Duncan. Just thinking of her brother made Ethan sigh. He'd been his closest friend, and he'd asked Ethan to care for his sister if something should happen to him. Now Duncan was dead, and soon, Meghan would be too.

Ethan's arms tightened around her naked body and she sighed contentedly. He couldn't help but damn himself for bringing her to the castle in the first place. If he'd left her to her grief, none of this would have happened. Then again, if it hadn't been for Meghan, the Dragon's Flame would have remained buried indefinitely, waiting until some other unfortunate soul found the gem within the Dragon's Death Mountains.

Ethan kissed the top of her head and closed his eyes, trying to calm his nerves and follow the Remembrance bond to the Crystal of Mynos. Malnan had said King Kaas's mages would be able to link to the Crystal in just such a way. He needed to see for himself if he could indeed talk to it through her. With Meghan sleeping, she was blissfully unaware of it all.

A strange fluttering touched his mind and his heart leapt. *"Hello?"* he asked mentally, feeling foolish for trying to talk to the talisman.

"Hello..." a ghostly voice answered.

Instantly, Ethan snapped open his eyes, taking in deep breaths, trying not to disturb the woman sleeping in his arms. The voice was barely audible, as if from far away, but he knew the Crystal was only held in Mynos's lair underneath Castle Templestone. Perhaps the fact that he wasn't bonded to it himself made it sound so faint.

"Are you the Crystal?"

Many voices seemed to fill his head all at once. *"Yes, Sir*

151

Ethan." Chills raced up and down his arms. The Crystal knew his name?

"I must ask you to let Meghan go. Release her from your bond."

"I cannot," the talisman whispered, its voices overlapping each other. *"I must fulfill my task of saving my Master."*

"You mean Mynos?"

"Yes."

"If you let Meghan go, then you can bond to anyone. Your task would be much easier. King Kaas has an entire army of mages!"

"None of them are women, Sir Ethan. I cannot ignore my enchantments. Mynos ensured that only the hand of a woman can touch me and live."

Damn. He'd forgotten that. *"What of Malnan? She is a dragon, her power would be greater than that of Djendorl if she wielded you."*

"Malnan will not risk hurting her mate. She will not use me to fight against him."

"But I thought you can't hurt him," Ethan said.

"You are wrong. I can hurt him, if Djendorl has possessed his body. My power cannot hurt Mynos, but I can distinguish between his soul and Djendorl's, despite whose body their souls are housed in."

"Then it would be possible for you to harm him if it was Djendorl's soul you encountered in his body."

"Yes. My enchantment follows Mynos's soul, not his body."

"What of Meghan? Why can't you sever your connection with her?"

"The bonding is a process I cannot stop, my son. The moment Meghan touched me, I bonded to her, and I cannot let

her go until this is finished."

"But she'll be dead by then!"

"Perhaps," the Crystal whispered. *"But there is no way for me to wield my power if I do not have a vessel to channel the magic through."*

"You're telling me you won't *let her go?"*

The talisman was silent a moment before it answered. *"You are correct."*

Ethan pulled his mind back as he stared angrily out the window at the night sky. His chin trembled and his hands shook with rage. He suspected the Crystal *could* let Meghan go whenever it felt like it. Unfortunately, it somehow understood the gravity of their situation and chose not to.

If only he had the Emerald of Estriel. For a brief moment, he entertained the idea of fleeing with Meghan into the wilderness of Lyndaria, never to be seen again. But Ethan loved his king and his country too damn much to be a traitor. No, he was a loyal Wolverine with every fiber of his being. He wasn't about to run away.

There had to be a way to ensure that Meghan wouldn't die. He doubted the Crystal could sustain her life while wielding its magic at the same time. Perhaps it *was* hopeless.

But one thing was for sure. If Meghan died saving Mynos from the clutches of Djendorl, then Ethan would die as well, whether in battle—or from a broken heart.

Chapter Twenty-Two

Malnan was exhausted. Standing on the battlements of Castle Templestone, she gazed out upon the pounding surf and sighed deeply as the night breeze played through her hair. She desperately wanted to shift and take flight, allowing the cool wind to clear her mind. But King Geoffrey had been adamant. No one was to enter or leave the castle with the threat of Djendorl looming over them.

Despite the fact that Djendorl had been sighted over the City of Krey hundreds of miles to the east, it didn't mean a thing. The dragon was capable of magic, and therefore could open a magical portal at any moment to attack the castle. They *must* be ready for anything. Geoffrey couldn't afford to have Malnan absent if something untoward should happen.

Another weary tear slid down her cheek and Malnan wiped it away. With all the tears she'd cried, it amazed her she still had more to shed. Her tear-shaped lavender Jewel hung around her neck, a habit she'd gotten used to after Sebastian and Jewel had brought her back from the cave within the King's Mountains.

She'd been killed a second time by Lord Merric of Westchester, but her soul had been able to once again bond to the body of the ancient embryo inside one of the three dragon eggs that had been hidden within the cave for millennia.

Malnan wondered whose cave it had once been, but it hardly mattered. Now, the only dragon who had ever cared for her was gone, possessed by a mad, bloodthirsty creature she herself had trapped within the Dragon's Flame.

Looking down at her Jewel, she turned it in her hand. It glittered in the moonlight. It was not enchanted like Mynos's Crystal—it was the vessel for her soul, refusing to let her drift into the afterlife. Her Jewel was the only reason she was alive. As long as she had a dragon's egg to breathe her essence into, she could never truly die.

At that thought, Malnan cocked her head and stared directly into the talisman. A wild idea struck her and her heart raced. Turning from the battlements, Malnan made her way briskly through the bailey of the castle. She was headed to Mynos's cave to see if her idea would work. With any luck, she'd confront Geoffrey in the morning with a wonderful new plan.

For now, she'd let the king of Lyndaria sleep in the comfort of his wife's loving arms. With a battle steadily approaching, he needed all the rest he could get. And Malnan knew all too well the peace a mate could bring to a tortured soul.

ᖇ

Arianna watched her husband with a worried eye. The very moment he'd stumbled into bed, he'd fallen asleep. He hadn't wanted to go rest, but Arianna had insisted none too politely, reasoning with him that he wouldn't be able to rule Lyndaria if he was asleep on his throne.

Geoffrey's handsome face was slack in sleep, but deep lines marred his skin and dark circles shaded his eyes. She didn't envy the burden he had to bear. She knew he felt guilty for the death of the villagers in the City of Krey. If he hadn't sent

155

Mynos to destroy the Dragon's Flame, then Mynos wouldn't have been cursed. Arianna had tried to ease Geoffrey's conscience, telling him he couldn't have known. But it hadn't much helped.

His dreams were troubled as he tossed his head on the pillow. Arianna laid her hand on his forehead and closed her eyes. The familiar warmth of magic flowed through her arm, smoothing the wrinkles on Geoffrey's face. He took a deep breath and sighed, cracking open his eyes, looking years younger. A muscle ticked in his jaw as he looked up at her, tucking a stray hair from her face.

"Thank you," he whispered.

"You deserve it." She smiled. "After what you've had to endure, you needed to be refreshed."

Geoffrey sighed again and stared at the ceiling. The pink glow of dawn poured through their window, bathing his profile in soft light. "What am I going to do, Rose?"

Arianna stroked his face. *"You're going to lead this country to victory."*

"I'm not sure I can."

"I am."

He gazed at her and pulled her onto his chest. "At least *you* have faith in me."

"You are my king." She gave him a gentle kiss on his skin. "And you are my husband. I'll stand behind you no matter what you have to do, and that goes for your men as well."

Geoffrey said nothing as he combed her hair with his fingers, but she felt the turmoil within his heart as clearly as if it were her own.

"The Wolverines love you, Geoffrey," she said, laying her chin on his chest. "They'd follow you into Hell if you gave the order."

"I know," he said, his voice cracking. "That's exactly what I'm afraid I must do. If Djendorl can bring an entire city to its knees, what hope do *we* have against him?"

"We have the hope of Kaas's army."

With a nod, Geoffrey said, "A hope that doesn't come without a price. Meghan will die, there's no way around that now."

Arianna bit her lip and she shivered. "I know."

"Imagine, Rose," he breathed, his eyes glistening. "Imagine if it were us. Ethan and Meghan are in love, bound by the Remembrance, just as we are. And yet they have to make such a horrible sacrifice... I could not watch you die."

Taking his face between her hands, Arianna scooted even closer to him, her eyes burning. "I had to watch *you* die once."

"This is different."

"No, it is not. You died to save me, to save our kingdom from Iruindyll. But I brought you back, I saved you."

"Because you are a fool," he said with a grin, pulling her lips to his for a quick kiss.

"Geoffrey..." When she didn't immediately finish her sentence, she felt his concern through their bond.

"What is it, Rose?"

"When...when Kaas's army destroys the Flame, Meghan will die once the magic flowing through her is spent."

Geoffrey nodded.

"Her bond to the Crystal will finally be broken."

"What are you getting at?" he asked mentally.

"I...I want to...help Ethan and Meghan." He raised a brow and bid her to continue. "Perhaps I can...bring her back."

157

Geoffrey's look darkened before he shook his head. "No."

"But I am the only person who's ever successfully brought someone back from the dead. I brought *you* back."

"Once. You were successful once." Geoffrey's eyes bored into hers, and she knew he referred to their infant daughter, who'd died in her womb. Arianna had tried to follow her into death's domain as well, but her contractions had scattered her concentration. She'd lost their daughter.

"It might be the only way..."

"No, Arianna. You touching Mynos's Crystal is what killed our little girl in the first place. I am not about to have you bonded to it again and spoil our chances of ever having an heir." With his words, he rolled over and rubbed her belly. "Rose, we are no longer just a simple farm girl and a knight of the king. We are *royalty*. We cannot risk our lives as frivolously as we once did in the past. We have a duty to this kingdom to protect it and protect its royal house."

Arianna looked away as a tear escaped her eye, trailing its way into her hair. "We cannot simply do nothing."

He hooked his finger under her chin, bringing her gaze back to his. "I am not saying no merely because you are my wife and I love you. I am saying no because you are the queen of Lyndaria. If you succumbed to the call of death yourself..."

Sorrow flooded through Arianna's heart and she knew he was thinking of what would happen to him if she should die. His fear was palpable, nearly choking her.

"Rose, I will not take that chance. Not for this kingdom, nor for my own sanity."

With a sigh, she conceded that he was right. If Lyndaria lost its queen on the heels of losing so many souls in the City of Krey, it would be too hard a blow for the people she now ruled.

Hugging Geoffrey close, she knew he must leave soon to make preparations for the siege that was sure to come. The prospect of fighting Djendorl in Mynos's body chilled her to the bone. She needed reassurance that everything was going to be all right.

"I must go," Geoffrey whispered. "I've rested enough."

Just as he was about to pull back the covers, Arianna stopped him. "Wait."

He looked down at her, hearing her thoughts. "Sweetheart, I cannot dally any longer."

She ignored his words, leaning up to place open-mouthed kisses along his neck and shoulders. "What of that heir you so casually mentioned a moment ago, my king?"

Arianna smiled the moment his resolve crumbled and he joined her once again in the pillows. "You have corrupted me."

"I have not," she breathed. A gasp escaped her at Geoffrey's bold caresses. "You have corrupted yourself by falling in love with me."

He chuckled, and the sound of it raised every hair on her body. "Indeed."

Chapter Twenty-Three

As dawn crested over the ocean, Mynos railed against his confinement within his own body. Reaching for his weaves of magic, he used them to push and strain against Djendorl's soul, trying to regain the upper hand.

Djendorl had spent the entire night laying waste to the countryside of Lyndaria. Farmlands burned, villages leveled, and all the while, the evil red dragon delighted in it all. Mynos had screamed the entire night, trying to get Djendorl to see reason, to keep him from taking the life of another innocent person. But he hadn't cared. And now, Mynos's own belly was full—with their remains. That thought alone made Mynos push so hard with his magic, Djendorl faltered in the sky.

"Why, Mynos," he chuckled. "Are you trying to unseat me?"

A pressure settled on Mynos's heart, and he knew Djendorl was using his own magic to suppress him. Seething, Mynos struck back, sending his magic from his mind in a pulse, creating a shock wave so strong, the air rippled around them. The dragon tumbled, falling to earth in his confusion. Mynos knew Djendorl hadn't been prepared for such retaliation, but Mynos had had enough. During the night, Djendorl had opened a portal to the coast, intent on burning his way to Castle Templestone. All the while, Mynos had flexed his magic, exploring Djendorl's link to the Dragon's Flame for any sign of weakness.

Perhaps he'd found it.

Mynos focused his own soul into the Flame, then lashed out, just as Djendorl had the moment he'd touched the gem. Mynos felt his strength returning to him. Beating his wings, he glanced at his scales. They shone golden in the light. His heart fluttered wildly and hope lit within him like a burning torch.

Then something hit him. Hard. Once again, the dragon faltered as Djendorl fought against Mynos for supremacy within his body. They tumbled through the air, and try as he might, Mynos could not release the Flame from his talons.

"You will *not* win this, worm!"

With Djendorl's words, a piercing magic stabbed Mynos's brain and he cried out in agony. His defenses down, he fell like a stone, and once again his body was overcome by the bloodthirsty beast.

He watched helplessly as Djendorl turned his scales red, beating his wings frantically mere seconds before they hit the ground. His feet alighted in the dirt an instant before he tensed and sprang back into the sky, flying with speed and agility.

"Oh, you will pay for that, *my king*. With blood!"

Mynos found himself praying to the Father of Dragons for the first time in millennia. Djendorl had to be vanquished, but Mynos obviously couldn't do it on his own. He prayed King Geoffrey was prepared for whatever the red dragon was planning. Without the strong magics of his brethren to stop him, Djendorl was almost invincible.

And he would have absolutely no mercy.

CB

Anger this hot hadn't burned inside Djendorl's belly since Biyanti's death. If he could, he would kill Mynos without a second thought. But killing him would mean forfeiting his body, and Djendorl wasn't ready to do that just yet. Mynos had caught him off guard by temporarily regaining control. That would *not* happen again.

Djendorl channeled his magic into the Dragon's Flame, erecting a barrier of sorts, between his soul and the gem. Mynos would not be able to bust through it. It would take much more than his puny attempts at magic to bring the mighty Djendorl down.

Just then, something caught his eye, and Djendorl spotted a ship riding the ocean waves just off the coast. Its sails were full of wind, sailing to some port of call. As soon as the dragon rounded a small rise in the countryside, a sprawling port city gleamed before him. Resplendent in the morning light, the city was beautiful.

"Djendorl, if you destroy Morcard—"

"You'll destroy me?" Djendorl laughed, delighting in Mynos's naiveté. "I'm already dead, Mynos. What can you possibly do to me?"

Swooping low, Djendorl didn't hesitate. He released his breath in a thunderous plume, engulfing every building in its wake, but he no longer hungered—for food. He now hungered for destruction.

With a wide grin, he circled the city for another pass, and relished the shrieks of his king inside his head. Before too long, the port city of Morcard was bathed in fire. Glorious fire.

CB

King Kaas had barely cracked an eye before someone shook him once more. It wasn't his wife Loara, as she had stayed behind in the elven kingdom. Then who was rousing him so early in the morning?

Sitting up in the large bed he'd been offered within the royal apartments, Kaas gazed into the eyes of a familiar elf.

"What news, Kerean?"

"Your Majesty, another scout has just portaled to the castle from Morcard, one of Lyndaria's northern port cities. Djendorl has been spotted laying waste to the city—as we speak!"

"What?" Kaas bolted out of his bed, searching the floor for his discarded robe.

"Would you like me to fetch your man?"

"Yes, wake Rowan. Tell him to meet me in Geoffrey's study."

Kerean bowed a moment before racing out the door to Kaas's apartments. Once Kaas found his robe, he flicked his hand in the air and opened a magical portal himself. Stepping through, he was relieved to find King Geoffrey already sitting behind his desk at this early hour, poring over paperwork. He barely looked up.

"What is it, Kaas?"

"Another report has come in, Your Majesty," the elven king said gravely. "I've just received word Djendorl has been spotted. He's destroying the city of Morcard this very moment."

Geoffrey's expression flashed with shock and fear before he masked it. "Morcard is a mere twenty miles to the north."

"We must awaken Meghan *now*." Kaas regarded Geoffrey with a critical eye. "My army cannot waste any time. We need to enchant each of them to her with the Remembrance before the dragon descends upon us."

With a sigh, Geoffrey ran his fingers through his tousled

hair. "Do it."

Kaas bowed slightly and turned on his heel, just as Rowan burst through the doors of the study. "Come with me, Rowan," Kaas said without breaking his stride. Rowan fell into step beside him.

"The dragon has been spotted. You must rally the mages. Waste no time."

Rowan gasped, but nodded. "Yes, Your Majesty." He dashed down the corridor, intent on his task. Once Kaas came to the Grand Staircase in the foyer of the castle, he took them two at a time and hoped his army had time enough to prepare before all hell broke loose.

Chapter Twenty-Four

Meghan startled awake when a thunderous banging echoed throughout her chambers. Ethan leapt from bed, pulling on his breeches while growling under his breath. Who was disturbing them so early?

"Wait just a damn minute!" he yelled, rubbing his face. Meghan lay back into the pillows and threw her arm over her face to shield out the bright sunlight streaming through her window.

Ethan didn't bother pulling on his tunic, he simply stomped to the door and yanked it open angrily.

"What?"

It was King Kaas. The elf didn't wait for an invitation. Stepping over the threshold, he glanced at Meghan. She sat up, trying to cover herself.

"It is time," he said, looking at Ethan. "Djendorl has been spotted." Ethan's face paled, but he nodded once, grabbing his tunic off the floor and throwing it over his head.

"Where?"

"Morcard."

Meghan gasped. "Then we...we don't have much time."

Kaas once again looked at her. "No, we do not. We must hurry before the dragon attacks the castle, Meghan."

A cold terror settled within her and she couldn't keep her arms and legs from shaking. Bile rose into her throat. It was hard to swallow past the lump that had formed. She nodded, standing from the bed and pulling the blanket with her.

"I...I will be ready in just a moment."

"Do not waste any time," Kaas breathed. "I shall wait for you in the hall." The elven king closed the chamber door behind him.

Meghan stared at Ethan. How could she possibly say goodbye to this man? Today was the day she would leave him forever—the day she was going to die. She marched to the bureau, yanking it open and choosing a pale pink gown, her eyes stinging with unshed tears. She couldn't help her trembling hands as she dropped the blanket, trying in vain to pull on her undergarments.

She hadn't heard him walk up to her, but Ethan's hands slipped around her bare waist, holding her back to his chest in a firm grip. He didn't say a word, but he didn't have to. He was scared. His fright radiated through their bond, and she knew he could feel her own fear.

"Be strong, Meghan," he whispered in her ear. Those three words cut the silence like a sword. A sob escaped her and Ethan's arms tightened.

"I don't know if I can do this."

"Yes, you can," he said, gently kissing the side of her neck. "You're a survivor, Meghan. We'll get through it."

She couldn't answer him.

"You lived through your parents' death at the hands of the Dark Knights. You've lived through your brother's death at the hands of Lord Merric. Meghan, you'll live through this."

"I don't believe I will."

Ethan turned her in his arms and gazed deeply into her eyes. "Stranger things have happened," he told her with a hopeless grin. "I have to believe you'll survive."

"You need to prepare yourself—"

"No. Don't talk like that."

Meghan held on to his shoulders and gave him a tearful smile. "All right." She knew his confidence was only denial. Ethan knew as well as she there was no hope for her life. But she needed to believe she was sacrificing herself for a greater purpose. Hopelessness would not help Mynos, nor would it help Lyndaria. She *must* believe in herself.

Standing on her toes, Meghan embraced him, rejoicing in the feeling of his warmth on her bare skin. "I love you, Ethan."

His entire body shuddered at her words and his sorrow stabbed her heart. *"I love you, too."*

"Stay with me?" she pleaded in his mind. *"Until the end?"*

A sob tore from his throat and he simply nodded. Meghan wished she could soothe his tortured heart, but she had to prepare for battle.

The dragon was coming.

CЗ

Geoffrey patrolled the battlements of Castle Templestone himself, making sure they were well fortified. Sebastian had done a marvelous job arming the men and positioning them on the walls, but the king would have expected nothing less from his Captain of the Guard.

On the fields surrounding the castle, Kaas's massive Army of Magi was preparing as well, having already broken camp and formed ranks. Chills raced up Geoffrey's arms and he prayed to all that was holy they had a chance against the dragon. He remembered the carnage Mynos had created on these very fields a few years before, decimating Queen Darragh's army with his fiery breath. Now, they faced Djendorl—without Mynos—and the fear of the unknown almost overwhelmed him. Even the hope of linking Kaas's army with Meghan's mind to wield the Crystal didn't soothe his nerves. She was going to die and there was nothing anyone could do to stop it.

Sebastian ran up the steps on the side of the wall and saluted Geoffrey. "We are ready, Your Majesty," he said, somewhat out of breath. "As ready as we can be, all things considering. Now we wait for Meghan."

With a nod, Geoffrey looked out across the countryside and heaved a sigh. "I hope it will be enough," he murmured.

Without warning, a magical portal opened a few feet away on the battlement, revealing Malnan, who stepped through almost immediately. "King Geoffrey!" Her eyes were wide with what looked like excitement, all the while she clutched her lavender Jewel to her chest.

"Malnan, what is it?"

"Your Majesty, Meghan does not have to die."

Geoffrey's brows shot up in shock at her words. "But we need her to wield the Crystal's power."

"And she shall. But she will also be holding my Jewel."

"I do not understand."

"My Jewel was never enchanted as the Crystal. It was merely a vessel to house my soul. But a thought came to me last night, and I enchanted my talisman for the first time since its creation."

A small hope lit within Geoffrey's heart. "With what?"

Malnan smiled. "When one holds my Jewel, they cannot

die."

Geoffrey's eyes widened and his mouth dropped open. Words escaped him in that moment, and all he could think to say was, "Are you serious?"

The dragon nodded, handing him her talisman. "No matter what happens, as long as she's holding the Jewel, her soul cannot leave her body for the afterlife."

Geoffrey took the gem and gazed at it in wonder. Turning it in his hands, he marveled at its beauty as it glittered in the sunlight. "It will not hurt her?" he asked, glancing back at Malnan.

"No. It will save her life."

Geoffrey laughed out loud. "Finally, some good news! Ethan will be overjoyed to hear this."

"Indeed, Your Majesty," Malnan said, chuckling herself.

Taking a deep breath, Geoffrey grabbed Malnan in a strong hug. "Thank you," he whispered.

"You are more than welcome."

He didn't know what lay in store for them in the hours to come, but Meghan's life didn't have to be sacrificed for the good of the kingdom after all. That news alone was enough to put a bounce in his step as he turned to find Ethan, and Duncan's sister. Perhaps there was some hope to be had after all.

CB

Ethan didn't want to take any chances. Along with Firefury, he strapped Duncan's sword, Swiftgleam, to his other hip as well. It was odd, carrying two swords, one on either side of him, but he'd be damned if he let that dragon anywhere near Meghan. If he had to fight Djendorl himself, he would be prepared.

Meghan said nothing as she watched him buckle her brother's sword belt to his waist, but she didn't have to. Her thoughts gave her away. She was terrified, and a little sick at the prospect of what she had to do. Asking her to forfeit her life was too much to ask. Setting his jaw, Ethan determined not to let her die. He had no idea how he could stop her death, but he'd find a way, damn it. Even if it killed him.

Once they were fully dressed, he opened the door and allowed Meghan to step through first, noticing Kaas waiting for them across the hall.

"Ethan! Meghan!" Spinning on his heel, Ethan spied King Geoffrey approaching them with a wide grin on his face. "I have excellent news."

"What is it, Geoffrey?" Ethan asked.

"Malnan has enchanted her Jewel for the first time since she created it. Meghan does not have to die!" The king grinned and handed her the gem. "If she holds it while wielding the power of the Crystal, its magic cannot kill her."

Ethan's eyes widened as a slow smile spread across his face. *"She won't die!"* Geoffrey's excitement was contagious. Ethan grabbed his king in a tight hug. In his elation, he even kissed Geoffrey on the cheek.

Relief permeated Ethan's entire being, and he whooped for joy, whirling to grab Meghan in a hug not too unlike the one he'd just given Geoffrey. She laughed in his ear, and the sound of it was the most beautiful sound in the world.

Setting her back on her feet, he took her face in his hands and kissed her soundly, only vaguely aware of the chuckles of the two monarchs in the hallway with them. Meghan's response fired his blood, and he felt as if he were floating on a cloud. She wasn't going to die today. Thank *God.*

"When I see Malnan, I'm going to kiss her into oblivion," he said mentally to Meghan, grinning like an idiot.

Meghan giggled at his thoughts while wiping away her tears. *"So am I."*

"Come," Kaas said, interrupting their silent banter. "We must retrieve the Crystal from Mynos's lair and meet my army on the field as soon as we can."

Meghan turned to the elf with a nod, her face beaming with exhilaration. "I am ready."

Squeezing Ethan's hand, Meghan barely flinched when Kaas opened a portal in the hallway that led to the cavern underneath the castle. Without a thought, she crossed the threshold with the man she loved, prepared to meet any threat Djendorl might throw at her. She wasn't going to die today. As long as she held Malnan's Jewel, she was immortal.

Let the dragon do his worst.

Chapter Twenty-Five

Holding the Crystal of Mynos in the palm of her hand was intimidating, and Meghan swallowed hard in an effort to calm her raging heart. Despite the knowledge she wouldn't die, it didn't mean she couldn't be hurt. That realization came to her the moment she'd touched the Crystal once again.

Its many voices had invaded her mind and she'd stumbled from the force of it. Their cacophony was almost painful, but having Ethan there to hold her steady relieved her somewhat. The Crystal was like ice, cold and unyielding. The Jewel, which Meghan clutched in her other hand, was warm in comparison, and both gems pulsated with their own inner glow.

Her hands shook with trepidation, the understanding of what she was about to do finally hitting her with full force. She was immortal as long as she held the Jewel—that much was true. But the magic Kaas's army planned to wield through the Crystal would, no doubt, be the most painful thing she'd ever had to endure.

"Are you all right?" Ethan asked, smoothing her hair away from her face.

"I'm terrified."

"I'll be with you," he whispered, kissing her temple. "Even to the end."

Meghan took a shaky breath and attempted to smile at him. Words escaped her while her body shook, and she nervously chewed on her lips.

"Meghan," Kaas said, his voice echoing throughout Mynos's cave. "I will first enchant you to me with the Remembrance. Once I am established in your mind, I can then harness the Crystal's power and bond my troops to you all at once instead of one man at a time. Are you ready?"

She nodded, despite her roiling stomach. Kaas placed his hand on her head and closed his eyes, chanting in a language she did not understand. After a few moments, Meghan slowly began to feel another presence in her mind—not too unlike Ethan's.

"Kaas?" she asked mentally.

The elven king smiled. *"I am here."*

Ethan's eyes widened and Meghan knew he'd heard Kaas's thoughts as surely as he could hear her own. This would indeed be an odd experience.

"Let's get above ground as quickly as possible," Kaas said aloud. "We cannot afford to waste any more time."

Once again, another magical portal stretched into existence, seeming to tear a hole in reality. On the other side were the fields that surrounded the castle, populated by hundreds of elven mages. Ethan placed his hands on Meghan's shoulders and squeezed. Their warmth seeped through her skin and gave her the courage she needed to step through the doorway.

Once they were all on the other side, the portal consumed itself and disappeared. Being outside the protection of the castle walls was unsettling, but Meghan refused to think about that now.

Kaas didn't say another word, he merely channeled his

magic through their bond, searching for the Crystal. It felt like water flowing through her limbs, weighing her down, making her gasp. It didn't take long for Kaas to find the call of the Crystal, and soon, the talisman burned brightly in her hand with the glow of magic.

Without warning, a shock wave emanated from the gem, and it changed from ice cold to burning heat within a moment, but Meghan didn't dare drop it now. She was experiencing only *one* elf's magic. No doubt it would become much more intense once the *entire army* channeled their power through her. She cried out in pain, but continued to clutch the Crystal, hoping Kaas would soon be finished.

Ethan said something, but what it was, she couldn't say. Her ears were ringing and she stumbled when the world tilted. A heavy weight bore down on her chest and it was hard to draw breath. But before she collapsed on the ground, it was over, and countless thoughts of hundreds of elves whispered their way through her head. It was almost unbearable.

She couldn't keep her head from spinning. Meghan fell back, finally succumbing to the sanctuary of inky blackness.

Cଷଗ

"It is done."

Ethan glared at the elven king. Was he mad? Patting Meghan's cheeks, he tried to revive her. She'd fainted shortly after Kaas had finished his spell, bonding her to his massive army. She still held onto both the Crystal and the Jewel in an iron grip, as if she couldn't let go of them. Perhaps that wasn't too far from the truth. Ethan had no idea what the effects of flowing magic were doing to her body.

Relief poured through him like rushing water when she

opened her eyes, trying to focus on him.

"Meghan? Can you hear me?"

She barely nodded, but did nothing to stand. He sat on the ground and placed her head in his lap.

"Can she handle wielding the power of your army, Kaas?" he asked, his voice strained. "She fainted with only *your* magic flowing through her."

"She will have to, Sir Ethan," the elf answered, a look of concern on his face. "It will be painful and trying for her, but we *must* be victorious!"

Swallowing hard, Ethan glanced down at Meghan's face and gave her a smile. "You'll be all right, I promise you. But don't you dare let go of Malnan's Jewel, you understand?"

"Not a chance," she breathed, attempting to sit up. Once she did, she clutched her head. "They're so loud."

Kaas knelt in the grass next to her. "That is something I cannot help with. It is the effect of the Remembrance that you hear and feel the thoughts of those you are bonded to."

"I see flashes... So many memories. So many feelings."

Kaas nodded and helped her to stand. "Do not think of that now. I need you to concentrate and try not to lose consciousness. It is paramount for us to destroy the Dragon's Flame."

"I understand. I did not faint until after your magic was spent." She reached out to Ethan. He steadied her by letting her lean on him fully. "I believe I can stay focused until the magic weaves are gone."

Shouts resonated from the battlements of Castle Templestone. Ethan turned to look only to see his fellow Wolverines yelling and pointing to the sky. Time stopped as he followed their gaze. Djendorl in Mynos's body was approaching from the north. Every hair stood on end as Ethan took in Mynos's red scales. He suddenly remembered his family, burned to death by Djendorl in the City of Krey. Many emotions raged through him at once, anger, sorrow, and an intense resolve not to let anything happen to the woman he loved.

Kaas yelled to his men, his voice presumably amplified through the power of the Crystal. "The time has come. *Shield!*"

Meghan cried out but stood her ground, her eyes closed with a look of concentration on her beautiful face. Instantly, a white light filled the sky, and Ethan could only assume they'd shielded themselves.

"Do not lash out until we can see the Dragon's Flame!" Kaas ordered, his eyes on Djendorl.

Ethan's skin prickled with awareness. Stepping in front of Meghan, he pulled Swiftgleam and Firefury from their scabbards, both swords blazing forth with a dazzling light from being so close to the power of Mynos's talisman. They hummed, as if they were excited for the fight.

As the dragon approached, Ethan heard the thoughts of Kaas's mages trickling through his bond with Meghan. They were confident of their impending victory. Their assurance bolstered his courage, and he planted his feet firmly on the ground.

He wasn't going anywhere.

Chapter Twenty-Six

The sight of Kaas's Army of Magi chilled Mynos to the bone. Spread out in formation upon the fields before the castle, he knew they must be shielded. He'd felt the shock wave of their magic—a wave only an army of that magnitude could create.

But regardless of their magic, Mynos feared for their safety. Unless Queen Arianna had once again taken up his Crystal, he doubted the elves would be able to fight Djendorl and win. Even now, the red dragon had succeeded in blocking him from retaking his body, no matter how hard he projected his soul through the Dragon's Flame.

Djendorl chuckled, seeming to hear his thoughts. "It appears the king of the humans has seen fit to welcome us. Shall we exchange pleasantries?"

Mynos didn't answer. It was pointless. Djendorl was determined to rain hell down upon Lyndaria and everything Mynos held dear. Instead, he concentrated on focusing his magic once again through the tainted red gem.

"Give up, Mynos," Djendorl said. "You know as well as I that it is hopeless. You cannot save them."

As they approached the army on the ground, Mynos spied King Geoffrey's Wolverines on the battlements of Castle Templestone, many holding bows and arrows aloft. The light of enchantment was upon the arrowheads, telling him Kaas had

had the foresight to strengthen their effect with magic. But the Wolverines did not let their arrows fly. Perhaps they were waiting for the army to strike first.

"Look at them, my king!" Djendorl yelled against the wind, seemingly giddy at the prospect of destroying an entire army of mages. "They actually believe they will be victorious."

A flash of light on the battlefield caught Mynos's attention. There, standing in front of the army, was Meghan, holding his Crystal aloft as if offering it up to the heavens. Sir Ethan stood in front of her, wielding two swords and watching the dragon approach with unflinching bravery. But Mynos didn't have time to wonder about that.

Djendorl inhaled mightily. With a few more wing beats, he was upon the army, spewing his fire along their ranks. But the flames skirted around a dome of magical energy without harming a single soul in its wake.

Mynos felt his rival's amazement as if it had been his own. He couldn't help but smile inwardly. He knew exactly what Kaas had done. Meghan couldn't wield the Crystal on her own—but Kaas's army could. He'd linked their minds with Duncan's sister, much the same way Iruindyll had done millennia ago during the first war for his talisman. Now Mynos understood how their shield had withstood Djendorl's breath.

With a deep growl, Djendorl turned in the sky for another pass. Mynos couldn't resist taunting the red dragon when he felt Djendorl's uncertainty.

"You are no longer quite as confident, are you?" he asked dryly. *"Perhaps they* will *be victorious after all."*

CB

With a great roar that shook the countryside, Djendorl flew

low, keeping the army in his sights. Summoning his magic, he cast as he flew, throwing air forward in a great pulsing surge, crackling with electric energy. The spell fizzled against the elves' magical shield. Djendorl growled and changed his tactics.

With two more beats of his wings, he was upon the castle, flying over the bailey. He hadn't taken another deep breath, so the fires in his belly weren't ready to spew forth. Instead, as he passed a tower on the battlement, he slammed it brutally with the end of his tail.

The roof of the structure collapsed, sending stones and bodies raining down into the courtyard of the castle. Screams and cries echoed in his ears, making him smile cruelly. Before this was over, the king of Lyndaria would curse the day he ever crossed the mighty Djendorl.

The archers on the walls released their arrows, and he deftly avoided most of them as he once again swooped over the fields. A few stuck in his hide and stung with the bite of enchantment, but they wouldn't be enough to bring him down. These humans were pitiful if that was the best they could do.

Inhaling deeply, Djendorl didn't bother with the shielded army. He was going to attack the castle and watch with glee as the structure crumbled to dust before his very eyes.

C8

King Kaas had held his army at bay long enough. It was odd, seeing Mynos's body gleaming red in the sunlight rather than gold, but it only served as a reminder that this was not Mynos they were fighting. Djendorl had already tried to demolish them with his breath and magic, but to no avail. The mages' power focused through the Crystal was enough to keep the magic of the dragon at bay. Even Kaas marveled at the

Crystal's ability to magnify the strengths of those who wielded it.

With his tail, Djendorl had brought down one of the towers along the battlements within moments. If Kaas didn't act fast, Djendorl could do unspeakable damage. Channeling through the Crystal, Kaas yelled at his men, amplifying his voice.

"Strike!"

All at once, the mages began summoning their magic, casting a spell designed to stun the dragon rather than kill him. White-hot light shot from the Crystal in Meghan's hands straight for Djendorl, striking him in the left flank. The dragon screamed in the sky and faltered for only a moment before righting himself. But he'd already flown past the castle, unable to inflict any more damage.

Kaas felt a sliver of hope enter his heart. If his mages could keep the dragon away from the castle long enough to bring him down, they might have a chance to destroy the Flame before this battle was through.

Djendorl was already flying erratically. It wouldn't be much longer now.

☙

"Report!" King Geoffrey's scream was almost engulfed by the shouting amongst his men, who were scrambling along the wall with their bows to get a clear shot at the dragon. A familiar face stopped in the crowd, his eyes wide. Geoffrey called out to him. "Cederick!"

The burly man dashed to where Geoffrey stood, glaring at the sky. "Sire, I came to find you."

"How many are injured?"

Cederick wiped blood from his forehead. "I do not know. But Sebastian was in that turret when it fell!"

Geoffrey's heart stopped, then slammed back to life almost painfully before he sprinted past Cederick down the steps to the courtyard. "Is he all right?" Geoffrey glanced over his shoulder, relieved to find Cederick had followed him.

But before Cederick could answer, Geoffrey saw Sebastian's injuries for himself as two Wolverines struggled to pull him from the rubble. His leg bent at an odd angle and dark red blood stained his tunic and breeches. Sebastian shrieked in agony when his leg hit a nearby stone. "Dear God," Geoffrey exclaimed. "You there!" He pointed to Sir Briand and Sir Joshua, who held Sebastian.

"Yes, Your Majesty?" Briand shouted.

"Take him to Queen Arianna. Tell my wife he needs to be healed."

"Right away." Both men bowed before hoisting Sebastian to rest on their shoulders. Without another word, they made their way back to the castle.

"King Geoffrey!" A woman's voice rang throughout the bailey. Glancing to his right, the king spotted Malnan running toward him, her green hair in disarray. "Your Majesty, I must help. You cannot fight Djendorl on your own!"

At that moment, a bright streak of light shot across the sky, striking the red dragon on his rear flank. His screeching roar rattled the men, but despite their obvious fear, many surrounded their king with swords drawn. Geoffrey couldn't help the surge of pride he felt in his Wolverines.

The light of the sun went dark for a split second as the great dragon flew over the castle, but even Geoffrey could see Djendorl had been wounded. King Kaas's army had done some damage with their magic, but it wasn't enough.

"You do not have the resources to battle a flying enemy," Malnan reasoned, dropping her gaze back to his eyes.

"But you are not as powerful as he is."

She nodded, her face grave. "There is that. But I believe I might be able to talk to him, get him to see reason."

"Malnan..."

"Your Majesty, I *must* insist. He has my mate." Geoffrey stared at her speechless for a moment. "Imagine if it were Queen Arianna he held prisoner. Would you sit idly by and watch events unfold? Or would you want to take part in winning her back?"

"We cannot risk losing you as well, Malnan," Geoffrey said.

The green dragon shook her head. "Do not worry about me, Highness. If I am killed, my soul will return to the Jewel. There is yet one more dragon's egg hidden in the King's Mountains. I will be able to return."

Geoffrey arched a brow. He hadn't thought of that. Djendorl let out another soul-searing bellow, and Geoffrey nodded. "Go. But do not do anything foolish."

Malnan didn't waste any time before turning to sprint up the stairs of the battlements. Geoffrey wondered what she had a mind to do. But before he could ponder her actions any further, Malnan leapt from the wall, into the sky beyond.

Chapter Twenty-Seven

As soon as Malnan's feet left the ledge of the battlement, she began to shift, spinning her magic to change her body into her true form. Green leathery wings ripped off her gown and grew from her back while long sharp talons sprang from her fingers. Her tail stretched out behind her and green glistening scales covered her skin. Within mere seconds, Malnan had once again become a dragon.

Beating her wings furiously, she rose higher in the sky, hovering over the castle, watching Djendorl all the while. He was circling the fields, as if uncertain what to do next. But she felt his mind in hers as sure as she felt the wind in her face.

"Ah, Malnan. Beautiful Malnan. I knew you couldn't resist meeting me again after all these years."

"Release Mynos," she demanded.

He laughed at her. "That is something I will not do. He is mine. As are you."

The red dragon flew closer, deftly avoiding the magic of Kaas's army. Again and again they tried to hit him with their fiery bolts, but Djendorl was too agile, twirling and looping in the sky with such finesse that even Malnan gasped at the sight. She had forgotten his prowess with flight. Djendorl had perfected his magical ability to help him fly, making him one of the lithest dragons ever to grace the skies of Lyndaria.

As he approached, she could feel his beckoning call. He was trying to win her with his abilities, the same way he had called to Mynos to touch the Flame in the Mountains of the Night. It was hard to ignore. The more she listened, the more she wanted to do exactly as Djendorl commanded. Shaking her head, Malnan channeled her own power to shield her mind.

"It won't be that easy, worm.*"*

Malnan spread her wings and sprang upward, tapping into her magic to push her body straight up into the clouds. Just as she knew he would, Djendorl followed not too far behind. His fiery breath engulfed her, but it did not burn. Her own abilities protected her, but her shield wouldn't hold for long.

Higher and higher Malnan flew, darting through the clouds as if she didn't have a care in the world. She didn't know what she was going to do other than keep the red dragon away from Castle Templestone long enough for King Geoffrey to regroup his men and tend to the wounded from the collapsed turret. But even now, Djendorl was gaining on her and she knew she'd run out of time.

Turning sharply, Malnan folded her wings close to her body and dove straight for the ground, using magic to propel her even faster than gravity could pull her. Her body pierced the clouds, leaving holes in her wake. Glancing over her shoulder, she saw Djendorl, hot on her tail, his face that of her beloved Mynos. It took her aback for a moment, as the face she remembered Djendorl having ages ago was not the same face he had now. He'd changed Mynos's glorious golden scales to a burnished red, but that was the only difference. He looked exactly like her mate and her heart ached inside of her.

"You are mine, Malnan. You are the last female of our kind. You will bear my wyrmlings."

"You are mistaken, Djendorl," she yelled back at him. *"I*

cannot bear your wyrmlings."

"Mynos cannot stop me from taking you."

"That may well be," she replied while plummeting to earth. *"But I am already pregnant with Mynos's offspring!"*

The great dragon roared behind her and seemed to double his efforts, reaching out his claws to grab hold of her tail. Malnan rolled in the sky, trying to dislodge him, but she was too close to the ground to do anything other than attempt to gain altitude once again. But Djendorl wouldn't have it.

His grip was stronger than she'd anticipated—he must be enhancing his strength with his magic. Without knowing what else to do, Malnan took a deep breath and released her deadly fire directly into the face of the dragon she loved.

♋

Meghan was screaming. Or at least she thought she was. Again and again Kaas and his army channeled their combined forces through the Remembrance bond, wielding the Crystal's power to lash out at Djendorl. Her arms burned, yet no fire consumed them. Her legs threatened to buckle, and yet, she somehow miraculously managed to remain standing.

Glancing at her own skin, she could have sworn she was glowing. Was she? Meghan didn't know for sure. Clutching Malnan's Jewel to her chest, she vowed not to drop it. The Crystal was draining her life energy, she could feel it. Every time the Army of Magi wielded their magic, she became weaker, more tired. And the pain was almost unbearable, as if her body were burning from the inside out.

The only comfort she found was in the warmth of the Jewel. It lent her strength when the Crystal stole it, and kept her racing heart from exploding within her. The pain was so fierce, she couldn't even form tears. Her eyes burned like the rest of her, but were devoid of any moisture to offer her solace.

Ethan stood before her, watching Djendorl like a hawk. She wanted nothing more than to be back within the shelter of his arms, feeling his mouth against her skin, and bask in the pleasure only he could create. But those thoughts were torn away as another pulse of magical energy swept through her, demanding more of her, forcing her to succumb to the will of the army, to the will of the Crystal.

Opening her mouth, she once again screamed at the top of her lungs. But whether or not any sound emerged, she had no idea.

Once Malnan and Djendorl shot upwards into the clouds, Kaas ordered his army to hold their offense. The moment their energy ceased flowing through her veins, Meghan collapsed, and slowly, ever so slowly, she closed her eyes, only vaguely aware of someone's arms around her. She hoped it was Ethan. Her sweet, loving Ethan...

CB

"Meghan!" Ethan dropped both swords and turned just in time to catch her as she fell to the ground.

"Sir Ethan, what has happened?" Kaas demanded.

"She has collapsed again. This is too much for her, Kaas. We're killing her!"

"She cannot die as long as she holds the Jewel."

"I don't care what Malnan has enchanted her talisman with. This is killing Meghan, can't you see that?"

"This is not killing her," Kaas said. "Draining her, yes. But not killing her."

"She cannot take any more of this! We must stop."

"If we stop now, Sir Ethan, Djendorl will win this fight. Is that what you want?" The elf's ancient eyes rested upon him and Ethan was struck with uncertainty. They had to defeat the dragon, but did they have to do it at Meghan's expense? *Damn it!*

He stroked her cheek and she moaned, seeming to snuggle deeper into the palm of his hand.

"Ethan?" Her voice was loud and clear inside his head, despite the fact that she hadn't opened her eyes.

"Yes, my love," he answered, his eyes stinging. *"Can you stand?"*

"I...I..."

"Get her up," Kaas ordered. "Malnan and Djendorl are returning!"

"Meghan, you must stand. You must wield the Crystal. We cannot defeat Djendorl without you."

She merely moaned in response, tossing her head this way and that.

"Sir Ethan!" Kaas yelled.

"I cannot get her to respond. She's overwhelmed. This is madness!"

"This *madness* will become chaos if that dragon attacks us without the Crystal's power to keep him at bay!"

"Meghan." Ethan shook her in desperation as the dragons screamed behind him. "Meghan, you must get up. You have to!" She opened her eyes. They were glazed over, but she seemed lucid. Without waiting for her to answer, he stood, pulling her with him.

Ethan turned just in time to watch as Malnan breathed green flames into Djendorl's face. The red dragon ducked just in time and swiped at her with his talons, tossing her across the sky. Malnan didn't have time to recover before Djendorl pounced, crashing into her with his lethal tail. He caught her wing and Malnan went down, disappearing beyond the cliffs, tumbling toward the churning waters of the ocean far below.

Kaas's eyes widened with fear as Djendorl wheeled in the sky, turning his eyes on the vast army before him. "Ethan!" Kaas screamed.

In desperation, Ethan kissed Meghan, trying to elicit a response from her. Within moments, she returned his kiss, and blessed relief washed through him.

"You must be strong, Meghan. I am with you. Be strong for me."

Pulling away from her, he nodded at Kaas, who once again commanded his army to shield themselves just before Djendorl heaved his breath once again. The fire was harmless as it bounced off their magic. The dragon had apparently had enough.

Beating his wings, Djendorl alighted on the ground and sauntered forward, intent on attacking them head on. Ethan watched as Kaas and his mages concentrated, summoning a giant ball of fire right before his eyes. As soon as it formed, it shot forward, streaking straight for the dragon. But before it hit his reddened scales, it exploded on an invisible barrier.

Djendorl continued to advance, his own shield holding up under the onslaught of the army's power. Ethan didn't even think twice. With Meghan once again on her feet, he stooped and picked up the swords he'd dropped in the grass. He'd kill that damned dragon before he harmed one hair on Meghan's head. But suddenly, Djendorl stopped, shaking his head. Right before his eyes, the dragon's scales turned from red to gold.

"Kaas," the dragon cried. "It is me, Mynos! Strike the

Flame. Now! I cannot hold him."

The elven king looked shocked, and that one moment of hesitation cost them dearly. The dragon's scales once again turned red and Djendorl screeched with fury. Even from where he was standing, Ethan could see the anger burning hot within his eyes.

The dragon sprinted forth, snapping his jaws, just barely missing them. Ethan hadn't realized how massive Mynos's body truly was until now, but that didn't stop him from bringing his swords down upon Djendorl's snout. In the commotion, Kaas and his men attempted to blast the red ruby clutched within his talons. But again, their magic dissipated along Djendorl's magical armor.

The dragon conjured his magic and hurled it toward Ethan in a streaking bolt of lightning. But it, too, fizzled upon Kaas's shield.

"I might not touch you with magic, boy, but I will kill you with my bare hands!"

Djendorl's gritty voice raised the hair on the back of Ethan's neck. It definitely wasn't Mynos talking. The air around the evil dragon's body shimmered like a living being as he shifted into his human form, looking like Mynos, yet having red-hued skin and dark red hair. Even his familiar slitted eyes were red. Without hesitation, the dragon strode forth, seemingly unafraid of Ethan's two swords.

Ethan smiled. A dragon he might be, but Djendorl was no match for his steel. He saluted the dragon before taking a fighting stance. Djendorl grinned himself, licking his lips as if Ethan were going to be his next meal. Perhaps that was exactly what he was thinking.

"I'm going to kill you, dragon."

"You kill me, you kill Mynos."

"It matters not. By now, Malnan must be pregnant. The pride of the dragons will live on."

Djendorl chuckled. "I just *killed* Malnan."

"I don't believe it," Ethan taunted. "You threw her down the cliffs, but she is not dead. Even I know it takes much more than that to fell a dragon."

Djendorl pounced, seizing the moment to use his powerful magic to blast Ethan's swords from his hands. Before Ethan had even seen him move, the dragon's human hands were around his throat, crushing his windpipe.

"You are no match for me, *Wolverine*," Djendorl whispered in his ear.

Ethan panicked. He'd vastly underestimated Djendorl's abilities. With one quick snap, the dragon could easily break his neck. *Oh God. Is this the end?* He closed his eyes and waited for his death to come.

Chapter Twenty-Eight

Kaas knew the instant Djendorl shifted he could no longer order his army to pummel the dragon with paltry magics. The spells needed to be lethal, not stunning. At this point, even killing Mynos to save Lyndaria was better than doing nothing at all.

His decision shuddered through his ranks, but he ignored their laments. Every one of them loved the golden dragon almost as they loved him. But Mynos wouldn't want them to hesitate just because his life was on the line. Kaas was certain of that.

Concentrating on casting, Kaas couldn't allow himself to be shocked when Djendorl grabbed Sir Ethan by the throat. He could only hope they'd complete the spell before the dragon snapped the Wolverine's neck like a twig. But in that moment, Djendorl's skin once again turned golden, and Mynos emerged, releasing Ethan immediately. Ethan crumpled to the ground, coughing and gasping for air. Mynos turned his pleading eyes on Kaas.

"I cannot let go of it, my friend. You must do it. You must finish this!"

Mynos's hands trembled and the Flame flashed in his palm. His skin's hue changed from gold to red back to gold again. Glittering tears formed in Mynos's eyes. "Tell Malnan to name our son Trisdan."

Kaas's own eyes misted as he nodded, watching Mynos's skin change once again. Before he had time to think, Kaas let his army's spell loose—a streak of deadly black lightning—hitting the dragon square in the chest. Djendorl flew back a few hundred feet before crumpling to the ground, lifeless.

Kaas immediately sprinted to where the body lay. Taking in the dragon's red skin and hair, Kaas was convinced he'd done the right thing. Djendorl had indeed conquered Mynos within his own body. Holding out his hand, the elven king chanted once again, this time concentrating on the Dragon's Flame still clutched in Djendorl's limp hand.

A massive shock wave emanated from Kaas's palm, pointed directly at the evil talisman. Again and again the shock wave pounded the gem, making the ground beneath his feet rumble with the force of it. Before long, the entire countryside resonated with a deafening roar as Kaas channeled more and more energy through the Crystal of Mynos.

The Dragon's Flame cracked under the pressure, the sound of it echoing all around him like a clap of thunder. Kaas didn't stop his magic, but continued to channel it, and within a few seconds, the gem turned black just as Djendorl's final, ethereal screams pierced the air. Fisting his hand, Kaas concentrated on fully destroying the Flame. It didn't take long before the talisman crumbled in upon itself, until it was nothing more than blackened dust blowing away in the cool breeze.

Once the gem was no more, Mynos's body returned to its golden hue, but he did not get up.

And he never would again.

C3

King Geoffrey had watched the entire encounter from the battlements of the castle. He'd been helpless to do anything more than watch as Kaas and his army defeated Djendorl once and for all. But it would appear that victory did not come without a price.

He bounded down the steps in the wall two at a time, his heart in his throat. He raced to the castle gates, ordering them to be opened at once. As soon as they rumbled aside, he sprinted through, with no less than thirty Wolverines to accompany him. His men weren't taking any chances with the protection of their king.

But once Geoffrey reached the site of the battle, his worst fears were realized. The great and mighty Mynos was dead.

CB

Ethan crawled to Meghan lying on the ground. His throat still hurt fiercely, but Meghan didn't appear as if she would awaken any time soon. She'd crumpled soon after Kaas had destroyed the Dragon's Flame, surrendering once and for all to the deadly power of the Crystal.

He cradled her in his lap, making sure he didn't touch the Crystal while also securing the Jewel in the palm of her hand. He couldn't lose her. Not now. Not after all they'd been through.

But he needn't have bothered keeping the gems safe after all, as it appeared Meghan's hands had clamped around them. In all likelihood, he wouldn't be able to remove them without hurting her. Ethan sighed and stroked her hair, talking both out loud and silently to her. He didn't know if she heard him, but it made him feel better nonetheless.

Her skin had a faint glow to it, probably an after-effect of all the powerful magic that had flowed through her body. She was unbelievably cold, and he tried his hardest to wrap his body around her to give her some of his body heat.

Kaas knelt next to them in the grass, smiling at Ethan through watery eyes. "We did it. Djendorl is dead."

Ethan's heart filled with sadness. "So is Mynos."

Kaas nodded. "Indeed he is dead, but he will not remain so."

Ethan gave him a confused look. "What do you mean?"

"I enchanted Mynos's soul when he released Djendorl's choke-hold on you, Sir Ethan."

Arching a brow, Ethan sat there in silence, waiting for the elf to continue.

Kaas cracked a smile. "I bonded him to Malnan's Jewel."

Ethan's eyes widened. "What? Don't you need to be touching it in order to bond someone's soul to it?"

"Normally, yes," Kaas said. "But you forget, when wielding the Crystal, my magic, and that of my mages, becomes hundreds of times stronger than it would be on our own. I was able to enchant Mynos's soul to Malnan's Jewel through the power of the Crystal."

Ethan glanced from Kaas to the gem in Meghan's hand. "So Mynos...is in there?"

Kaas nodded slowly, grinning from ear to pointed ear. "And there's one more dragon's egg in the King's Mountains."

Ethan's jaw dropped.

"Mynos may be dead, but he will not remain that way."

"And what of Meghan?"

Kaas's expression once again turned grave. "I'm afraid we can do nothing for her until Mynos can be reborn. He is the

194

only one who can release her from the bonding of the Crystal, and hopefully revive her body. It is true she did not die, Sir Ethan. But you were right. She didn't emerge unscathed."

At Kaas's words, Ethan couldn't hold back any longer. He broke down into deep, heart-wrenching sobs. "Please tell me she'll be all right."

"I don't know that for certain, my son. I truly do not know."

❧

Malnan awoke to sharp rocks in her back and wet surf pounding her scales. She'd tumbled over the edge of the cliffs with a broken wing, only to end up half-submerged within the pounding waves of the Silver Sea. Shifting into her human form, she cried out as her body's anatomy changed, pulling and tugging on her injuries. Her right arm hung limp at her side and it was all she could do to find the weaves of magic within herself to heal it. Wading to the short beach at the bottom of the cliffs, Malnan sat in the sand and waited until her body was fully healed by her magic.

"Malnan."

Glancing around, she saw no one, but she'd recognize that voice anywhere. "Mynos?"

"It is I, my love."

"Where are you? Are you all right? What of Djendorl?"

"King Kaas has destroyed the Dragon's Flame."

Malnan stood, her heart overcome with joy. "That is excellent news!"

"Malnan," Mynos said again.

"Yes?"

Her mate was silent for a moment before he said, *"In order to defeat Djendorl, he had to use his lethal magic. Kaas could not stun him."*

Malnan knit her brows together in confusion. "What are you saying?"

"I am dead, my love."

Malnan's head snapped up at his words, suddenly panicking. *"Dead?"* She began to shift once again into her draconic form.

"I am dead, but not forever. Kaas bound me to your Jewel. I can return!"

Once her transformation was complete, Malnan leapt from the rocky beach, climbing higher and higher until she crested the top of the cliffs. Flying low over Castle Templestone, Malnan made her way to the battlefield. Hearing Mynos's words about returning to her did nothing to ease the horrendous pain within her heart. Her mate was dead. She had to see for herself.

Lying in the grass beyond the castle was his body, still in his human form. Once Malnan had alighted on the ground, she shifted, using her magic to create a new, shimmering gown to cover her as she knelt next to Mynos, stroking his golden cheek. King Kaas and King Geoffrey gave her room to grieve.

"I have your word you will return?" she asked him.

"Yes," came Mynos's ethereal voice. *"We have but to find Sebastian and Jewel's cave once more."*

Malnan smiled as her emerald tears fell, dropping into the grass as tiny gemstones. She wiped them away, giving Mynos's lips a soft kiss one last time.

"I love you, Mynos," she whispered.

"I love you, too, Malnan," he whispered right back, his voice reaching her through her own soul's bond to the Jewel.

Swallowing hard, she took a deep breath and closed her

eyes, holding her hands over Mynos's body.

"What's she doing?" Ethan asked, still holding Meghan in his arms.

"Wait and see," Geoffrey said with a sad grin, his hands behind his back.

Within moments, Mynos's human body disappeared. The only thing that remained was a sparkling golden gem winking in the grass. Everyone present gasped at the sight, beholding for the first time the gem born of a golden dragon. Even Malnan hadn't been prepared for the beauty of the talisman her mate's body had created. It was bittersweet, consecrating Mynos's body, knowing he was dead, but also filled with the knowledge that he would return—soon.

Lifting the gem gingerly from the grass, Malnan stood and presented it to King Geoffrey. "Mynos wants you to have this," she said. Geoffrey took it reverently.

"What will you enchant it with?" he asked.

"I haven't yet decided, Your Majesty."

Chapter Twenty-Nine

With a saddened heart, Ethan asked Kaas to lift the Remembrance binding Meghan to his army. The elven king nodded and broke the bond a moment before removing himself from her consciousness.

"Thank you," Ethan whispered, still cradling her in his arms.

"No, thank *you*, Sir Ethan, for being so courageous. What you have been willing to sacrifice says volumes about your character."

Ethan sniffled. "I'm not willing, Kaas. God help me, but I'm not! I love this woman, and if she dies... If she *dies*..." He couldn't go on.

"She will not die." Kaas laid his hand on Ethan's shoulder.

"She won't awaken." Ethan was aware of how pitiful he sounded, but he was well beyond caring. "Meghan has given more of herself than anyone could have ever imagined. I want her back."

Kaas sighed, murmuring words to an elven spell. A portal opened in front of them, leading straight to Meghan's bedchambers. "Go. Be with her. She needs you now more than ever. You do not need to remain."

"What of Mynos?" Ethan asked, nodding toward the Jewel Meghan continued to clutch in her hand.

"Resurrecting Mynos can wait for another day."

Glancing at King Geoffrey and Malnan, he gave them a look of gratitude and stepped through the portal. Once on the other side, the magical doorway collapsed on itself, leaving Ethan alone with Meghan in his arms.

He walked to the bed and laid her upon the mattress, pulling the quilts back to give her some warmth. She held on to the draconic talismans so hard her knuckles were white. But no matter how much Ethan cooed to her, she would not open her eyes. He began to wonder if she ever would again.

"Don't leave me," he breathed, kissing her lips gently before lying next to her. He lost track of time as he lay there staring into her face, hoping to God the battle with Djendorl hadn't broken her soul.

As long as she held Malnan's Jewel, she wouldn't die. But would she ever again truly live? Hugging her close, Ethan hid his face in the crook of her neck and wept.

☙

Mynos was dead. Arianna could hardly believe it as she gazed at the golden gem within the palm of Geoffrey's hand. Tears threatened to fall from her eyes, despite the fact she'd already shed her fair share that day.

For hours, she'd been healing the injured, including Sebastian, who'd opted to spend the rest of the day with his pregnant wife. She didn't blame him. She knew he'd been frightened half out of his mind when the red dragon had destroyed the tower. It had come crashing down—with him inside it—and he'd confided in her that he thought it would be the last thing he'd ever see.

The queen heard similar stories throughout the day as she healed everything from a broken back to minor cuts. Now, however, seeing the talisman Mynos's body had created confirmed once and for all that the great, benevolent, golden dragon was gone.

But Lyndaria wasn't without hope.

As soon as Meghan awakened, Malnan would return to the cave in the King's Mountains along with her Jewel and Mynos would be able to breathe his essence into the last known dragon egg. But it wouldn't be the last egg for long. Malnan was pregnant, a fact Arianna's husband had been very upset over once he'd found out not too long before. Malnan had deliberately kept that information from him. If he'd known she was pregnant, he never would have allowed her to fight Djendorl on her own. If she'd been killed, only *her* soul would have returned to the Jewel, not those of her offspring, and the survival of dragonkind was too precious to gamble with.

Geoffrey's anger at her deceit still radiated from him as he held the golden stone, Arianna could feel it. He gazed at the dragon in his study with a critical eye. Malnan had just given the gem back to him after taking it once again, claiming to have enchanted it with a new power.

"I have called it the Dragon's Star."

"What does it do?" Geoffrey asked, turning it in the light.

Malnan smiled. "Think of Mynos's sister Estriel."

Geoffrey hesitated a moment before closing his eyes, trying to form an image in his mind of the silver dragon from the stories Mynos had once told. Suddenly, the image came to him, of a glowing silver dragon, dazzling in the morning light—as beautiful as she was graceful. He gasped at the sight within his mind.

"Now, think of the original war for the Crystal."

Clearing his mind, Geoffrey once again turned his thoughts to the stories he'd heard as a child, and a vast valley spread out before him, filled with mages, channeling their power as one through the Crystal, in much the same way Kaas's Army of Magi had done that morning. Scores of dragons fell from the skies and Geoffrey couldn't stop his groan of sorrow.

"Now think of something more recent—Lord Merric, perhaps."

Geoffrey made a face, but did as he was told, trying to conjure the image of the insane lord from his memories. Flashes of Mynos sprinting across a grassy courtyard emerged, and he saw Lord Merric in his sights, running like a madman before him. In the vision, Mynos fully shifted into his draconic form and took flight, snatching Merric into his mighty claws before gaining altitude over the bay of Evendria.

Opening his eyes, Geoffrey stared at Malnan in wonder.

"I have enchanted Mynos's gem with his thoughts, feelings, memories. Anything Mynos has ever done or seen is recorded within that talisman, along with his knowledge of magic."

Arianna stepped forward. Despite looking haggard and exhausted, she still took Geoffrey's breath away with her beauty. "You're saying the Star gives the wielder Mynos's memories?"

"That and more, Daughter," Malnan explained. "It will also allow them to wield Mynos's power."

Geoffrey stood speechless for a moment before saying, "It gives you the knowledge, wisdom and power...of a dragon?"

Malnan nodded with a slight grin. "And not just any dragon. Mynos himself."

Turning the gemstone in his hand, Geoffrey gasped at the

beauty of the many facets, seeming to glitter of their own accord. "Anything we want to know about Mynos's past—"

"And more importantly," Malnan interrupted, *"Dragonkind's* past. Mynos was our king in every way, Your Majesty. He knows more about our traditions and family line than any other dragon before him, even Djendorl, who was older and more powerful than he. But there is one thing I forgot to mention."

"What is that?" Geoffrey asked, reluctantly tearing his gaze away from the stone.

"It will not manifest its power for someone who is not pure of heart. If it ever falls into the wrong hands, it will be useless, as the talisman knows your intentions, even if you try to wield its power through a brainwashed pawn."

Arianna cleared her throat before she spoke. "Then it will be highly revered throughout Lyndaria. May I suggest we place it on display in the Great Library, Geoffrey?"

"Indeed. We should not keep the knowledge of a dragon from the people, if they wish to learn."

"You will need it, Your Majesty," Malnan said, pacing the room. "Once Mynos returns in the flesh, we shall find a place to birth our offspring, and I fear we may not return for quite some time. If it is true the Isle of Dragons is now below the waters of the Silver Sea, then it is up to us to find a new nesting ground for our sons and daughters."

Geoffrey nodded in acquiescence. "A few hours ago, before Kaas left the castle with his army, he wanted me to tell you something."

Malnan turned to give King Geoffrey her full attention. "And what might that be, Your Majesty?"

"Before Mynos...well, before he died, he asked Kaas to tell you to name your son Trisdan. Does that name mean anything to you?"

Malnan stared at him for so long, Geoffrey thought she might not answer. But when she did, her voice was no more than a whisper. "That was the name of Mynos's father. He fell in battle many, many years ago, leaving Mynos behind as the King of Dragons. Mynos always admired his father. There was never a question of what we'd name our son."

"How do you know you'll even have a boy?"

Malnan rubbed her belly and looked down, reminding Geoffrey of when Arianna had been pregnant, long before she'd lost their baby girl. That thought sent a pang of grief straight through his heart. He tried his best to hide it.

"Every first born of a golden dragon is a boy, King Geoffrey," Malnan said. "And that boy is a golden dragon himself. When he comes of age, our son Trisdan will be the King of Dragons, however miniscule dragonkind may be."

"Such wonderful news," Geoffrey said with a grin. He walked to where Malnan stood and gave her a swift hug. "Then you must take care of yourself. You are too important to the future of the draconic race to do anything rash now."

"I *will* take care of myself," she said, smiling at both Geoffrey and Arianna. "For once, I can say I am truly happy. And when Mynos returns, my life will be complete."

"You cannot say you haven't earned your happiness," Arianna said, also giving the dragon a hug.

"An understatement, to be sure." Everyone chuckled at Malnan's words, and Geoffrey found himself relieved that the Dragon's Flame had been destroyed. Now, all they needed to do was wait for Meghan to open her eyes.

Chapter Thirty

"Sir Ethan, it has been three days."

"I am well aware how long it's been."

Sebastian sighed with concern for his friend. "Perhaps it is best if you let her go."

Ethan looked at him sharply. His eyes were sunken and his clothing hopelessly wrinkled. Sebastian didn't think Ethan had even slept since the battle with Djendorl. He'd sat in a chair next to Meghan's bed for the past few days, constantly watching her, trying to get her to eat, and worrying himself to the bone. It would seem he hadn't given up hope she would open her eyes. Or at least, he hadn't accepted the fact that she might not.

Clearing his throat, Sebastian stood next to Ethan's chair and placed a hand on his shoulder. "Malnan wishes to start her life with Mynos and their offspring. You must let the dragon take her Jewel."

Ethan shrugged Sebastian's hand off. "If she takes the Jewel, Meghan will die."

"Is she even alive now?"

"She's alive," Ethan spat. "She is breathing. She is still with me."

"Only physically. Malnan, Arianna, Rowan... All of the most powerful mages in Lyndaria have examined her. They cannot help her. She's teetering on the edge of a knife, constantly at death's door, but never able to step through. Is that how you want the woman you love to spend the rest of her days? Do you want her to remain in a state that allows for neither death nor life?"

Ethan was silent for long moments. "She will awaken."

"You don't know that, my friend. As much as you tried to save her, perhaps now it is time you let her go."

"And what will that do to me, Seb?" Ethan yelled, standing so fast, he knocked the chair over. "If Meghan dies, so will I. We are bonded with the Remembrance! Once she's gone, I won't be too far behind."

"Malnan can lift the—"

"*No!* I do *not* want to be separated from Meghan. She asked me to be with her, until the end, and I intend to live up to my word."

"But she will never know. If you took the Jewel from her hand this very moment, she would never know."

"*I would know!*" Taking one step closer, Ethan stood eye to eye with Sebastian, staring him down. "*I* would know," he said in a calmer voice. Breaking eye contact, Ethan righted his chair and plopped back down, his shoulders slumping like a man defeated.

"Perhaps we should die together."

"Do not talk rubbish," Sebastian said, scolding him. "You don't have to die."

"Oh, but I'll want to." Leaning across, Ethan reached out to smooth Meghan's hair. "If Meghan isn't in my life, I no longer want to live it."

Sebastian chewed his lip and took a deep breath. He folded his arms on his chest and remained silent, knowing nothing he could say would make sense to this grieving man.

"It is the Crystal that's killing her," Ethan whispered, staring at Meghan's face as if committing every line to memory. "She cannot let go of it, and no one else can touch it. A cruel irony, don't you think?"

"Ethan..."

"If she could only let go of it, her direct contact with the talisman should be lessened enough for her to open her eyes."

"You don't know that."

Ethan gazed at him with haunted eyes. That look alone made Sebastian's heart break for him, wondering what he'd ever do should their roles be reversed. If Jewel had been consumed by the power of the Crystal, Sebastian would try to do everything he could to save her, or die right along with her. In that respect, he understood Ethan's pain.

"I have to try." Ethan glanced back down at the woman on the bed. Her hands looked like claws clutching onto the gems and her skin was pale. She took slow, shallow breaths, and Sebastian had to strain to even hear them. Meghan wasn't living as much as she was merely existing.

Ethan stood once more, only to sit on the edge of the bed.

"What are you doing?" Sebastian asked, taking a step closer. Even though Arianna had healed his wounds from the turret's collapse, his leg still managed to give him a twinge of pain.

"Saving her," Ethan said a moment before he grabbed hold of Malnan's Jewel. He didn't take it from her hand, however, he merely grasped it, just as she.

"Ethan? What are you..."

At that moment, a shock wave rippled through the room as a sickening reddish glow bathed everything with the light of enchantment. Sebastian only had a moment to be shocked before he'd realized what Ethan had done.

He'd touched the Crystal of Mynos.

Ethan screamed, a sharp, ear-piercing scream that seemed to split the air in two, but he pulled and tugged with his right hand, trying his hardest to dislodge the Crystal from Meghan's grasp. The cruel magic pulsing through his veins felt like boiling lava, bubbling through his body, burning everything in its wake. His vision turned red and his heart fairly exploded forth from his chest. Gritting his teeth, he dared not let go of Malnan's Jewel, or he would surely die as an effect of the Crystal's enchantment, as only the hand of a woman could touch the gem and live.

The veins on Ethan's hands and arms glowed red, and he couldn't help but wonder if there would be anything left of him once he'd loosened the Crystal from Meghan's hand. Stabbing pain sliced his head, seeming to shoot down through each of his limbs. With a shuddering cry, Ethan managed to pry the talisman somewhat from Meghan's fingers, and a dull ray of hope lit within him. But the pain was nearly unbearable.

Suddenly, his nose began to bleed, dripping onto the quilts of the bed. His ears and eyes also trickled with the blackened, viscous liquid.

"Ethan!"

He was barely aware of Sebastian's voice. He used all his strength to yank his arm back, finally releasing the Crystal from Meghan's hold. In awe and wonder, Ethan regarded the gem in his hand, flashing red, as if angry to be in the hands of a man. Without wasting another moment, he hurled it across the room, where it hit the floor with an ethereal ping before rolling to rest against the far wall.

He tried to wipe his nose, but his right arm was no longer working properly. The room whirled about his head and he couldn't get his bearings no matter how hard he tried.

"You're a goddamned fool, Sir Ethan of Krey!"

Sebastian's words sounded muffled, as if he were hearing them through water. Unable to hold himself upright any longer, Ethan crumpled to the floor, content to fall back into the pitch-black void of unconsciousness.

CR

"Geoffrey, wake up."

Cracking open his eyes, Geoffrey gazed into the face of his wife. "What is it, Rose?"

"I felt a shock wave. From inside the castle!"

That got his attention. He sat up so fast, his head spun. "What?"

"It had to come from the Crystal. I'm sure of it."

Geoffrey swept the quilts back and stood, looking for his robe. "How long ago?"

"Only a few moments." Arianna stood as well, grabbing her robe off a chair near the fireplace.

Once they were both decent, he tore open the door to their chambers and strode purposefully down the hall. A mixture of fear and worry filled him, making him quicken his stride.

"Geoffrey!" Sebastian raced down the hall toward him. "I was just coming to wake you."

"Arianna felt a shock wave, Seb. What's happened?"

"It's Ethan, Your Majesty. He touched the Crystal of

Mynos!"

Arianna gasped behind him and Geoffrey had to cover his mouth to prevent himself from doing the same. "What in God's name... Is he dead?" Geoffrey dreaded Sebastian's answer.

"No. He took hold of Malnan's Jewel before trying to wrestle the Crystal from Meghan's grasp. He thought if he could get her to let go of it, she would wake up."

Geoffrey broke into a run with Arianna close behind. "Has she?"

Sebastian kept up with them. "No."

"Summon Malnan!"

Sebastian immediately sprinted down the hall, intent for the grand staircase. Geoffrey and Arianna took the hall that led to Meghan's room. The king cursed Sir Ethan for being a monumental fool. But he couldn't say he wouldn't have done the same. He'd been just about as desperate to get Arianna away from the Crystal of Mynos not too long ago himself.

Once they reached Meghan's door, it was wide open. Malnan was already within the room, kneeling next to Ethan, her hands glowing white.

"You're here!" Geoffrey stood shocked in the doorway at the sight.

"I felt a shock wave. I portaled here before any more time was wasted."

"I just sent Sebastian to fetch you."

"No need. I shall call him back." Malnan closed her eyes for a moment, then nodded at him.

"How is he?" Geoffrey leaned over her shoulder to take a look. Ethan's skin was an unhealthy shade of grey, and every blood vessel under his skin was streaked with red. His breathing was uneven, and his entire right arm was blackened and useless. "Dear God."

"No man has ever touched the Crystal and lived, Your Majesty. He only survived because he held my Jewel. I'm afraid his injuries might be beyond my abilities to heal."

Arianna dropped to her knees next to Ethan, stroking his hair away from his face. Her fear was apparent as she looked back at the dragon. "I've seen the Crystal kill a man once," she whispered. "When I was on Shadow Mountain, in Iruindyll's stronghold. It was not a sight I ever expected to see again."

She sniffled, but continued. "His name was Stephan. He was a Dark Knight, but the Crystal burned him from the inside out. His veins glowed a bright red, much like Ethan's did, if this is any indication." She held up his arm to show Geoffrey and Malnan the pattern of his veins beneath the skin. "I cannot believe he still lives."

Geoffrey glanced at the bed, taking in Meghan's gaunt frame. "And it seems as if his sacrifice was for nothing. Meghan has not awoken."

Malnan shook her head gravely. "If there is a chance I can heal him, it is likely he will never again wield a sword."

Silence descended upon the room and Geoffrey had to wipe away a tear. "Saving his life is more important than saving his sword arm, I'm sure Meghan would agree. Do all you can for him."

The dragon gave Geoffrey a nod just as Sebastian ran back into the room with a few Wolverines in tow.

"Seb, help Malnan take Ethan back to his quarters."

"Yes, Your Majesty."

Sebastian strode into the room with Briand, Quinn, and Joshua behind him, who each grabbed a limb, lifting Ethan from the floor. Nothing else was said as the men carried him out into the hall. Malnan turned to follow, but Geoffrey stopped her.

"What of Meghan?"

The dragon turned her slitted eyes to the bed and sighed deeply. "She is no longer in danger of imminent death, Sire. Letting go of the Crystal has stopped its deadly effects for now. But I am uncertain if the magic that flowed through her during the battle has injured her beyond waking."

"Can she let go of the Jewel?"

Malnan considered his words before answering. "I believe so."

"Then we cannot delay in bringing Mynos back. I will send Sebastian to take care of it himself."

Malnan nodded slowly and he knew she was disappointed she couldn't take Mynos to the King's Mountains herself. Geoffrey took her hand in his.

"Malnan, I need you here."

"I know, Your Majesty." With one last look at Meghan, she whispered, "Bring him back to me."

"You have my word."

"One more thing," she said before she turned away.

"What?"

"The Crystal is on the floor in the far corner. Make sure no one touches it."

When her green eyes met his, a chill raced down Geoffrey's spine. In all the commotion, he'd forgotten about the Crystal of Mynos. With wide eyes, he said, "Understood."

♋

"He is failing faster than I anticipated." Malnan glanced worriedly into Ethan's face, taking in his sunken eyes and gaunt frame. He wasn't going to last much longer. The damage the Crystal had done was now slowly killing him.

"But he held your Jewel. How can he possibly be dying?" King Geoffrey leaned over the other side of the bed, having just ordered the Wolverines who'd carried Ethan to his quarters to go back and guard Meghan's door. He'd also ordered Sir Sebastian to take Malnan's Jewel and journey to the King's Mountains where the last dragon's egg was hidden. Soon, Mynos would return to the castle in all his glory.

"Holding my Jewel interrupted the enchantment that would have killed him, Your Majesty. Regardless that he held my Jewel, the Crystal's effects still injured him, in much the same way Meghan has yet to awaken. The power of Kaas's army has harmed her as well. But Ethan no longer holds my Jewel, and the damage that has been done will now take his life."

"Is there nothing we can do for him?"

Malnan shook her head. "Only Mynos has the knowledge to heal an enchantment such as this. I fear in touching my Jewel, Ethan merely delayed the effect of the Crystal for a time."

"Sebastian will return with Mynos very soon."

"True, but Sebastian has only just left. Even with the Emerald of Estriel to take him directly to the hidden cave, it will be many hours yet before Mynos will hatch after breathing his essence into the wyrmling within the egg. Ethan will be dead by then."

Geoffrey hissed an oath through his teeth and raked his fingers so hard through his hair, Malnan winced. "So now *both* of them will die? If Ethan dies, Meghan won't be too far behind from Remembrance poisoning."

"The Remembrance only poisons you if the person who lifts

the spell is not the one who cast it," Malnan argued.

"I beg to differ." Geoffrey made a sour face. "Arianna has told me many times what it was like after I had died near Iruindyll's fortress. She felt split in two, as if there was an insurmountable darkness surrounding her. I do not wish the same for Meghan and Ethan."

Malnan sighed, turning her gaze back to the pale man lying on the bed. Sorrow almost overwhelmed her at the thought of Ethan never being able to build a life with the woman he loved.

"Malnan?"

She turned to Geoffrey once more, curious at the look on his face. "What is it, Your Majesty?"

He glanced into her eyes and the faintest hint of a smile played on his face. "I have an idea."

Malnan cocked her head.

"The new gem you created from Mynos's consecrated body—that golden diamond. Didn't you say it had all the knowledge of Mynos housed within its depths?"

The longer she stared at the king of Lyndaria, the more Malnan began to realize where his thoughts were headed. No one but Mynos knew how to lift the effects of his Crystal. And they had his knowledge at their fingertips.

"That it does, my son." Malnan's grin grew almost as wide as Geoffrey's. "Perhaps this is the perfect opportunity to learn from its magic."

Geoffrey nodded. "I think you might be right."

Chapter Thirty-One

Meghan awoke screaming. Both fire and ice seemed to flow through her veins at the same time, while a deafening roar resounded in her ears. She tried to cover them to shield out the sound, but her arms barely lifted off the bed before dropping back to her sides. What was wrong with her?

After a few more moments of burning, frigid pain, it was gone, and Meghan breathed a sigh of relief. Moisture fell from her eyes and into her hair, but one thing held her rapt attention.

Silence.

The many voices of the Crystal of Mynos were gone, no longer plaguing her with their whispers. Even when she wasn't directly conversing with the talisman, they'd been there, ever present in her mind. Meghan hadn't realized until that very moment how prominent they had become.

She took another deep breath and opened her eyes, only to see the smiling face of Malnan looking down upon her.

"How do you feel?" the dragon asked.

"I don't hear it," she managed to say, even though her tongue felt thick within her mouth.

"Hear what, child?"

"The Crystal. It is gone."

The dragon's smile widened. "I have broken your bond with the Crystal. You no longer have any more ties to it."

Meghan's eyes widened in her shock. Attempting to sit up, she couldn't fully do so without Malnan's help. But after a short while, she was propped against the headboard, nestled amongst her pillows.

"It has released me?"

"No, Daughter, *I* have released you."

Meghan glanced at something that had caught her eye. Held in Malnan's hand was an unfamiliar glittering gem. Meghan couldn't remember ever hearing stories about a golden talisman. The dragon turned it in her hand and it flashed with its inner light, seeming to twinkle of its own accord.

As if reading her mind, Malnan said, "This is the Dragon's Star."

"It is beautiful!" Meghan stared at it in awe. Not even the Crystal sparkled so magnificently. It did indeed glitter like a star in the sky.

"It gave me the knowledge I needed to break your bond with Mynos's gem."

"I thought only Mynos had that power?"

Malnan bowed her head. "The Star has all the knowledge of Mynos within it. I was able to channel my magic through it and find what I needed to know."

Meghan furrowed her brow in confusion. "Did we defeat Djendorl?"

"Yes, child."

"Then where is Mynos?"

Malnan did nothing more than hold up the Star between them. "Here," she whispered. Meghan gasped.

"I don't understand. I thought a gem had to be born of the
215

consecrated body of a dragon." Her heart sank as the realization of what must have happened began to take hold. "Oh no... Mynos is *dead*, isn't he?"

The green dragon nodded sadly. "He was killed by Kaas and his army. There was no other way to break Djendorl's hold over Mynos's body. But all hope is not yet lost. Mynos himself will be reborn in the last of the ancient dragon eggs in the King's Mountains."

Meghan stared at the dragon in wonder. "Just as you were?"

"Just as I was."

Biting her lip, Meghan gazed at the gem once more. "He's so *beautiful*."

"That he is, Daughter," Malnan agreed with a small smile. "I do not believe Lyndaria has ever seen the effects of a consecrated golden dragon. The Star will serve to keep our draconic history intact. Whatever Mynos knew in life is contained within this gem."

"Amazing."

"I couldn't agree more."

Meghan glanced around the room just as her stomach rumbled loudly. "I'm so hungry." Clutching onto her stomach, she made a face.

"That is to be expected. You have been unconscious for over three days."

"Three *days*?" Meghan's jaw dropped. "Where is Ethan?"

Malnan looked away, but Meghan didn't miss the look that crossed her face. A cold dread shuddered through her. She tried reaching out to Ethan with her mind, but he didn't answer. She felt him through their bond, but he wasn't awake. But it was too much to hope he was merely sleeping.

"Malnan, tell me. Did something happen to Ethan?"

The dragon swallowed hard, then returned her slitted gaze back to her. "Sir Ethan grabbed hold of the Crystal of Mynos in an effort to save you from it." Meghan gasped, covering her mouth to keep herself from crying out. "You hadn't opened your eyes in quite some time and he'd become desperate. He took my Jewel in one hand and the Crystal in the other, wrenching it from your grasp. He succeeded in slowing your decline, as touching the Crystal had continued to drain your strength. My Jewel ensured that you would not die, but you weren't alive, either. Ethan merely tried to bring you back from the brink, and in so doing, he injured himself, perhaps beyond repair."

Malnan's words raised every hair on Meghan's body. Ethan had sacrificed his own health and safety to save her? She felt as if she were going to be sick. "Is he all right? I mean, is he... Did he..."

"For now, he is stable," Malnan told her, taking her hand. "I attempted to heal him with the Star before I broke your bond to the Crystal. I could not heal him completely, and I believe he will need many rounds of healing before he will fully recover. But I do not believe he will ever be the man he once was."

"What...what..."

Malnan squeezed her hand, offering her comfort, somewhat. "His right arm was badly wounded. If magic can't heal him, he might never regain the use of his sword hand. It is altogether possible Sir Ethan can no longer be a Wolverine."

Meghan let out a shuddering sigh. "My God. That will crush him."

"Yes, but he is alive. He is the only man in history to touch the Crystal and live to tell the tale since Mynos enchanted his talisman all those years ago."

Meghan nodded, wanting desperately to go to him. "May I

217

see him?"

"You are still weak," Malnan said. "Once you have eaten and can stand on your own, you may visit Ethan at your leisure."

"I do not feel like eating."

"You must to regain your strength."

Meghan sniffled and wiped her eyes. "Please don't let him die."

Malnan gave her a look of sympathy. "I will do all I can. I promise you that, Daughter, as the queen of dragons."

C3

Meghan didn't get out of bed until the next morning. Despite Malnan's healing magic, nothing worked wonders like a hot bowl of soup. But each time she moved, she winced, as every muscle in her body screamed in protest.

Getting dressed in one of her fine gowns took half the morning, and Meghan couldn't help but wish she'd never touched the Crystal of Mynos in the first place. The gown she'd chosen was pale yellow, given to her by Sebastian's own wife, Lady Jewel of Tabrinth. Just thinking of her made Meghan smile.

At one time, she'd been jealous of Lady Jewel for being the object of Ethan's affections. But how very wrong she'd been. Ethan had made it clear exactly which woman he fancied, and the memory of their lovemaking made her blush. She couldn't bear the thought of never feeling the sensation of his skin against hers for the rest of her life.

She had to clear her throat to keep from crying. She was going to see him today, and she'd be damned if he woke up to a sobbing woman. After all he'd been through, the man deserved her smile.

Meghan opened the door to her room only to find Malnan waiting for her in the hall. "Don't you sleep?" Meghan asked with a grin, closing the door behind her.

"Dragons don't need as much sleep as humans."

"What are you doing here?"

"I came to help you to Ethan's chambers. I know you are still sore."

Meghan nodded. "That I am. Perhaps if I lean on you just a bit?"

The dragon chuckled and handed her a large green gem. "I trust you know how to use this?"

"That's the Emerald of Estriel. I...I saw Ethan use it once when he first brought me to the castle. It takes you to places you've been before."

"Then you should be able to use it well. I will not be visiting long with Ethan."

"Why not?" Meghan gazed at Malnan curiously.

"My mate has returned." The dragon smiled, and Meghan's eyes misted.

"Mynos is *back*?"

"He is with Sir Ethan as we speak."

Smiling, Meghan closed her eyes and asked the talisman to take her to Ethan's room. A bright, thin line appeared in the hallway, stretching into existence before widening into a magical portal. Through it, she could see Mynos himself gazing down at Ethan, who lay on the bed. But his eyes were open. Ethan was awake.

With a squeal, Meghan hobbled across the threshold, wincing, yet grinning at the same time. Immediately, Mynos flew to her side, allowing her to lean into his human frame.

Grabbing handfuls of his tunic, Meghan hid her face in Mynos's chest and wept, unable to express the intense emotions coursing through her. "You're alive!"

"Yes, Meghan." Mynos's deep voice gave her goose bumps. "And so is the man who saved your life."

Meghan glanced at Ethan, who stared back at her with such love in his eyes, she could scarcely draw breath. Mynos somehow knew what she wanted, and led her to the bed. All she cared about was the man holding out his good arm to her.

"Meghan! Dear God, I never thought I'd hold you again." His voice in her head made her break down, and before Mynos had even let go of her, she latched on to Ethan, holding him as if her very life depended on it.

"I love you," she whispered over and over, placing kisses along his chest, his neck and his jawline.

"I love you too," he answered, cupping her cheek.

Ethan grabbed a handful of her hair and pulled her lips to his in a rough kiss, but Meghan welcomed it. She answered him in kind, holding on to either side of his face in an effort to keep him right where he was.

"Promise me you will never touch the Crystal again." Ethan's voice sounded tortured.

"As long as you promise me the same."

"I promise." He smiled, kissing her again.

Meghan rejoiced when his tongue darted along her lips, gently asking for entrance. Once she opened her mouth, he plundered, exploring her almost reverently. There was no doubt in her mind this man was in love with her—she felt it radiating through their bond. She held his heart, just as he held hers.

"Malnan and I have healed him a bit more from the effects

of the Crystal's enchantment," Mynos said from the other side of the room, having given them their privacy. "But Sir Ethan needs many more healings before he will be fully recovered."

"As long as he's alive, that is all that matters," Meghan said, stroking Ethan's cheek. He gave her a sad smile and she knew he was thinking how he could possibly remain a Wolverine knight. "What of his arm?" she asked Mynos, knowing full well Ethan wasn't going to ask him.

The dragon sighed, but his gaze remained optimistic. "He will most likely have trouble with it from time to time, during the wet or cold months. He will definitely have to train and train hard to regain strength enough to wield a sword. But if there's one thing I've learned through the ages, children, it's that *anything* is possible."

As Meghan watched Mynos and Malnan gaze at each other with their obvious love, she knew Mynos was right. Dragonkind should have been wiped out many times over, but the hope of the dragons stood before them now, ready to start their lives anew and rebuild their race.

"We will be taking our leave now," Malnan said, giving Meghan a knowing grin. "I do not know when you will see us again. We must find a suitable nesting ground for our young."

Ethan curled his arm around Meghan, holding her close. "Thank you, both of you, for all you have done."

The dragons bowed their heads before Mynos said, "I will be taking the Crystal with us. Don't bother looking for it."

Meghan rested her head on Ethan's shoulder. "I have no desire to look for it. I have all I need in my arms already."

Mynos smiled and Meghan's heart leapt at the sight. "As do I." He wrapped his arms around Malnan. "Farewell."

Ethan sniffled. "Take care of yourselves."

"That, Son, is a given." Mynos grinned.

With a bright flash of light, the dragons disappeared. When Ethan kissed her once again, Meghan sighed with contentment, and the entire world fell away.

Chapter Thirty-Two

"Mynos, are you sure you want to do this?"

The sweet voice of Malnan echoed throughout the cavern. He glanced at his mate, lying naked next to him. They were both in their human form, having spent their passion not too long before. They'd journeyed to the very cave Mynos had been reborn in, reveling in the knowledge they were finally going to have the children they'd always wanted. Hearing Malnan tell him she was pregnant again had been the happiest moment of his entire long life. She'd been pregnant once before, but Malnan had died in the Mountains of the Night before she'd been able to give birth.

Now, however, dragonkind had a true chance of rebuilding their numbers and Mynos couldn't wait for the day his daughters and sons would fly in the skies of Lyndaria.

"I am sure, my love," he whispered, holding his Crystal in the palm of his hand. The talisman sparkled, refracting its own glow as hundreds of tiny rainbows danced on the walls. "I have spoken with King Geoffrey. He agrees this is what must be done."

Malnan caressed his arm. Her touch never ceased to make him shudder. "But you've always loved Estriel."

Mynos nodded. "And now it is time to say goodbye. From the time I consecrated my sister's body, the Crystal has been sought after for ultimate power and greed. It cannot be allowed to fall into the wrong hands again, whether an insane dragon or an innocent young girl."

Malnan gave him a smile full of regret. "I am sorry. I know how much you longed for your Crystal to be used for knowledge."

"Now we have the Dragon's Star."

"That we do. With all the power and wisdom of the one I love." Malnan pulled his head to hers, giving him a tender kiss.

Mynos's eyes misted as he turned his sights back to the gem in his hand.

"*Mynos,*" the Crystal's ethereal voices whispered. "*It is time.*"

Taking a deep breath, he said, "Sleep well, sister."

Closing his eyes, Mynos channeled his magic directly into the talisman. The Crystal glowed brightly from the amount of power he wielded and he continued to increase its pressure until the entire cave around them quaked. Small rocks and dirt fell from the ceiling as Malnan took his other hand. He clutched onto it, trying hard not to let his emotions get the best of him. This was the end of an era, the end of a legacy, and Mynos mourned its passing. But now, he would forge ahead with Malnan by his side, with absolutely nothing to fear.

Within moments, the inner light from the Crystal went out, and its voices were silenced. The ground trembled one more time before Mynos squeezed his hand, crumbling the gem into nothing more than dust.

"Goodbye, Estriel."

Malnan cupped his cheek and leaned her forehead on his.

"You did the right thing."

"I know." Two drops of golden tears fell from his eyes, embedding themselves into the floor of the cave. He embraced his mate, ready to start a new day.

C03

"Marry me." Ethan stroked Meghan's hair, still marveling at its fiery color. This woman never ceased to amaze him, and he suspected she'd continue to amaze him every day of his life.

Round-eyed, Meghan lifted her head from his chest. "Are you..."

"Proposing? Yes, my dear. You should know by now I cannot live without you." He grinned when she did, and closed his eyes as she traced the lines of his face with her fingers. She suddenly shifted her body weight, crawling to lie on top of him on the bed.

"If I am to be your wife, Sir Ethan, there are a few things we need to make clear."

Snapping open his eyes, Ethan gazed at her with a raised brow. "Oh?"

She nodded. "Indeed. First, you must accept that your trysts with other women have come to an end. I will not share you."

"Not even with the Lady Jewel?" he yelped, as if shocked. Meghan smacked his shoulder, making him howl in mock pain. "Ow!"

"You deserved that."

He chuckled. "Perhaps I did."

"Secondly, you are to promise me you'll never do anything so stupid as to risk your own life to save mine."

"Oh, milady, that is a promise I cannot make." She pouted, but he kissed her before she could object. "I am a Wolverine, and I intend to stay that way. I will need your help to get back on my feet. But know this, Meghan. If you are in danger, I will do everything in my power to protect you, and that has nothing to do with the promise I made to Duncan. It is because you are the woman I love, the woman I want to bear my children, and nothing in this world is ever going to take you from me. Understand?"

Meghan bit her lip, but nodded. "I cannot lose you, Ethan."

"You won't lose me," he breathed, wiping his thumb across her lips. "Not to another woman, not even to death."

"Now you plan to cheat death?"

"Good God, yes!" They both giggled and Ethan basked in his happiness.

"Then my answer is yes. I'll marry you."

He shouted with joy and squeezed her close. "I'm not sure how much influence you'll have as the Lady Meghan of Krey, however," he said wryly through his grin. "The city *was* leveled after all."

Meghan smiled and ran her fingers through his hair. "Then we'll rebuild."

Ethan sobered, amazed by her words. "Perhaps we shall."

After that, no words were said as he claimed her mouth, wishing desperately he could make love to her. But no matter how hard he tried, he couldn't move much from his position on the bed.

"Do not worry yourself about that," Meghan's voice whispered in his head. Her hand was suddenly between them, tugging at the ties to his breeches. *"I will do all the work."*

With his good hand, Ethan reached up to unbutton her

gown. "Not *all* the work, my love," he said.

"Perhaps not," she answered, easing his breeches down his legs. Once they were shed, she helped him with her buttons until she was able to lift her gown over her head. Once his tunic and her undergarments were shed, she kissed him deeply, slicking his skin with hers. She melted in his mouth like the sweetest sugar. He'd never tire of tasting her.

Meghan whimpered when he lifted himself just enough to rub against her moist heat. He gasped at the sensation as well and fisted his hand in her hair. "Make love to me," he demanded, knowing full well she could both see and feel the depth of his passion.

Her answer was to kiss him once more, thrusting her tongue into his mouth as she lifted her hips. Ever so gently, Meghan eased down upon him, sheathing him fully with a cry of desire. She didn't need any encouragement as she rocked back and forth, bringing him steadily to a height he'd never experienced with any other woman. Again and again she took him inside, gasping at every plunge, striving for the pleasure he knew would consume her.

Once she fell over the edge, her body wrapped around his, caressing his hardened length within her depths. Ethan couldn't hold back any longer. With one final thrust, he came as well, kissing Meghan hungrily, holding the back of her head to make sure she couldn't escape him.

"I want forever, Meghan," he murmured against her lips.

"You have it," she answered without hesitation.

"I never thought love would hurt so damn much."

"If it didn't hurt, it wouldn't be real."

Ethan supposed truer words would never be spoken. He didn't think his heart would ever stop pounding whenever Meghan was near. But they had the rest of their lives together.

227

He was determined to prove to her and to himself that he would recover from his injuries. She had such tremendous faith in him, that it made him want to succeed—if only to be her hero.

"You are already my hero, Sir Ethan of Krey." She'd apparently heard his thoughts.

He blushed, but held her tight against him, his heart overflowing with love. "And in that, milady Meghan, I will never disappoint you."

Epilogue

King Geoffrey of Lyndaria, Ruler of the Four Realms and Leader of the Order of the Wolverine, lay in his enormous bed in the royal apartments with his head in his wife's lap. He sighed dreamily at the feeling of her fingers threading through his hair, and marveled that all he'd had to do that day was sign countless papers and writs from about the kingdom.

He couldn't help but smile, remembering when he'd hated signing documents all day, but no longer would he take such a mundane task for granted.

"Sir Ethan has been pushing himself to wield Firefury once more." Arianna's soft voice drifted down to him and he opened his eyes. She smiled and he couldn't help but think she was the most beautiful woman in the world.

"Yes, he has," Geoffrey said, remembering Ethan's display in the bailey a week ago. He'd been practicing with Sebastian, who'd been using every available moment of his free time to get Ethan back into shape. But Sebastian had been going easy on him and Ethan knew it. Once he'd demanded Seb didn't hold back, their sparring match had turned serious, and Geoffrey had been impressed by Ethan's tenacity. He survived longer than anyone thought he would, even impressing Sebastian with his prowess before Sebastian had swiped the sword from Ethan's hands.

But Meghan had never ceased to watch her new husband whenever he trained, to offer her support if nothing else. They had been married in a quiet ceremony not too long after the dragons had departed the castle.

"Lady Meghan has been pursuing me for funding to rebuild the City of Krey."

Arianna chuckled. "She's about as persistent as that husband of hers."

"You think?" Geoffrey chuckled as well.

"I, for one, think it's a fabulous idea."

"Indeed it is," he said, lifting his arm above his head, stretching.

"When do you think Mynos and Malnan will return?" Arianna smiled down at him.

"I don't know. But how strange it will be to see their children in the sky."

Arianna nodded. "And in the castle."

"Yes," Geoffrey agreed.

"They'll all be such good friends."

He nodded himself, then looked at his wife in confusion. "Who?"

"Our children, of course."

Geoffrey was silent as he arched a brow.

"Oh, you men can be so dense sometimes!" she exclaimed.

"Rose, what are you talking about?"

Arianna laughed when he gave her an exasperated look. "I'm pregnant, you silly oaf!"

The world stopped and Geoffrey sat up in a flash. "You're—"

"Pregnant, yes!"

His heart in his throat, Geoffrey tugged his wife into his

arms and howled for joy. "Are you sure?" he managed to choke out.

"I am sure," she said mentally. *"A boy."*

"A boy," he breathed, as if in prayer. "I'm going to be a father?"

"Yes!"

Geoffrey's joy couldn't have been greater as he laughed out loud and bounced on the bed. Hugging Arianna close, he whispered his love to her over and over again. Through his tears, he claimed her mouth, leaning her back into the pillows, determined to lose himself within her open arms.

In that moment, all was right with the world.

About the Author

Rebecca Goings has always enjoyed writing stories. As a young child, she wrote stories and poems to stay sane through her parents' divorce and the lonely years ahead. Her stories not only became her therapy, but they became her safe-haven as well. Knowing that becoming an author was her dream, Rebecca entered her stories and poems into contests and won a few awards. She wrote her first romance as a junior in high school and shared it with friends, who encouraged her that it was good enough to publish. But Rebecca decided to have a family first before pursuing her dream. She lives in Oregon with her husband, four kids, two cats, and a dog.

To learn more about Rebecca Goings, please visit www.RebeccaGoings.com. Send an email to rebeccagoings@gmail.com or join her Google group to join in the fun with other readers as well as Becka! http://groups.google.com/group/themagicofromance.

Between two races that hate each other, at the doorway between two worlds, can Claire find the strength to be the emissary they all need?

Go Between
© *2007 Dayna Hart*

Book One of The Curtain Torn series.

Halfway through her twenties, her divorce, and a bottle of rye, Claire opens her birthday present—a "pressed fairy" book.

One of the fairies is neither pressed, nor a picture. He's the sinfully sexy Dell, who's been trapped inside the book for twenty years. The moment Claire frees him, goblins attack her house. Dell and Claire's only option is to use a "Between"—a rift between their worlds—to escape into the land of Fae.

There, Claire discovers the elven queen, Eliane, has a mission for her—one that has her keeping secrets from Dell. And ousting the goblins from her home is only the start.

Available now in ebook from Samhain Publishing.

Enjoy the following excerpt from Go Between...

Claire smothered a gag that had nothing to do with the rye she'd been drinking. Glaring at the birthday gift, she cradled the bottle in her hand. So it was only a mickey. Claire was a cheap drunk. With her almost compulsive tendency to finish what she started, a forty in the house would have just been stupid. She wanted enough to ease her pain, not end up standing on her balcony, naked and screaming at passers-by. Not again.

The no-name cola she'd been using for mix sat on the coffee table, which suddenly seemed too far away. After a moment of consideration, she swigged directly from the bottle of rye. Her eyes burned, and her cheeks bellowed, but it stayed down. She grinned with a fierce pride. The smile froze when her gaze fell on the papers on the ottoman and the gaudily wrapped package beside them. Reminders of what had caused her to crawl into the bottle to begin with. One was her birthday present from Ryan. Not the overly festive package, either. No, her high school sweetheart and husband of five years had served her with divorce papers. On her twenty-fifth birthday. Not that the divorce was a surprise, they'd been separated for over a year, but as always, Ryan's timing sucked.

The only one whose timing was worse was her sister, Marielle. Because she had just opened the divorce papers when another messenger arrived. Carrying the package. Neon-green wrapping paper with tiny purple and aqua polka dots, tied with a huge hot-pink bow; it was the ugliest thing Claire had ever seen. And whatever was inside it could only be as bad. Maybe worse. Marielle had some strange ideas of what Claire wanted, and who she was. Past birthday gifts had included edible underwear, adult-only Twister, and fuzzy socks. In the same package.

The eye-popping paper didn't disguise the gift—it was a book. A big book. A heavy book. Yet, still, a book. But Claire couldn't help but wonder what kind of book it was. She'd spent an entertaining half-hour taking wild guesses. Her latest: a coffee table version of the Kama Sutra, with full colour illustrations. Bound in leopard-print velour. Claire studied the package again, letting her gaze trace the lines of it, too afraid to let her hands do the same.

Lifting the bottle for another swig, she checked the level of the amber liquid inside. Half empty. Or was that half full? She giggled. It didn't matter. Either way, she had half of a bottle to self-medicate with. If the book turned out to be the Nazi manifesto, bound in human skin, she'd have enough alcohol to drown the memory. The bottle tucked into the crook of her arm, Claire pulled the ottoman closer with her free hand. She hefted the book in her arms and debated putting it back, ignoring it, pretending it had never arrived. She knew Marielle would phone, though, asking pointed questions to make sure Claire had really opened the book.

Sighing, Claire tore off the ugly pink bow. Peeling away the wrapping paper, she stared in disbelief at the cover of the book in her lap. It was a Squashed Faery book. Each page featured a different illustration of a faery, supposedly pressed between the pages of the book like a flower. She traced the gold-embossed lettering of the title with one finger, a smile tilting the corners of her mouth. Warmth that had nothing to do with alcohol spread through her body. She and Marielle had gotten a similar book when they were kids, from some aunt they hardly knew. They'd spent hours staring at the pictures, giggling at the expressions on the tiny faces. With every turn of the page they would try to convince each other they'd seen one move before the giggles would set in again.

The happy memories made her feel worse as the reality of her current situation slammed into her. She was twenty-five. The middle of her twenties. The middle of a divorce. The middle of a crisis. She took another swig then put the bottle on the floor beside her. Peeling off the plastic that bound the book, she inhaled the familiar scent of paper, tainted slightly with the mustiness of age.

She stopped after listlessly turning a few pages and stared down at the book. Red, brown, green and gold leaves appeared to swirl across the page, as though being tossed by a gentle breeze. The male faery, wrapped in an autumn-red leaf, was almost invisible. His hands were outstretched, palms up, as though he was trying to push the pages off himself. His hair looked like spider webs fanned around his chiselled features, which were pinched with his efforts. Without those tiny hands, she might never have found him in the tumble of leaves. Peering into the book, she followed the line of his wide shoulders, down his chest to a narrow waist. Not badly built, for a Little People. Little Person? Claire considered that, reaching over the book to grab the mickey. Something bit her breast, and she jumped, the rye sloshing in the bottle, but not spilling.

"What the hell?"

A spider. Maybe an ant. She looked at the page, expecting to see some kind of biting insect skittering across the page. Never mind that in the midst of a Canadian winter, any bug but a cockroach would be hibernating. And the thought of a cockroach—especially one that might bite—was just too disgusting to consider. When she looked down, already inhaling to let loose a scream that would shatter a bug to pieces, there was nothing on the page but the little faery. His tiny hands were clenched into fists, and his chin jutted at her in defiance. Something about that wasn't right. She exhaled noisily and turned the page, then took another swig, her eyes closing against the fierce burn.

She opened her eyes in time to watch the page flip back to the one with the leaf-faery. Futile fury welled up in her chest. She'd told Ryan there was something wrong with the windows. Even when they were closed, a breeze came through the living room. This was proof. The brief moment of victory felt hollow, though. Ryan was across town at his girlfriend's place—not there to listen to her gloat.

She sighed, leaning away from the book to put the bottle on the floor beside her, checking it when it wobbled. Satisfied it wouldn't fall, she stared at the little faery. His fisted hands were outstretched, pushing up over his head, a thin layer of plastic bubbling up from the page with his efforts.

Wait. That wasn't right. She pulled the book up close to her nose to examine the faery.

"Are you going to sit there gawking, or are you going to help me out here?"

The book fell to her lap, and Claire watched the faery jostle across the page. She stared in disbelief at the faery standing in the middle of the page with his hands on his hips. She tilted the book to the left, and the faery slid across the page. She angled the book to the right, and he skittered that way, his feet skipping underneath him to keep his balance. When the book was level again, he turned his gaze onto Claire. "Would you stop that?" He stamped his foot in irritation.

"Oh, sorry," Claire said, but he wasn't listening. Reaching toward Claire, his hands pressed against the plastic, separating it from the page. His hands were far enough apart to create two separate bubbles with space between them. Claire thought they looked like pinchers. As his hands closed together, she realised she hadn't been bitten, but pinched. Part of her brain whispered she should be incensed, but she was too fascinated to work up much in the way of anger. She stared as he pushed one hand to join the other in its plastic bubble, straining his muscles to break free. But the plastic wouldn't give. It snapped back into place with a pop, and he sagged. Panting with exertion, he glowered up at her. "Could you give me a hand?"

Without thinking, Claire reached out to touch the page with the tip of her finger. Wiggling her nail a little, she felt the soft resistance of the bubble around the little man. With a final twist of her finger, her nail gouged the bubble. The man's hands burst through to grab her fingertip. Holding tight, he heaved himself out of the book, the plastic shredding around him. Once he'd brushed himself off, he stood astride the open pages with a triumphant grin.

"Much better, thanks!" He shook his head, which sent his silver hair fluttering around his face. Stamping his foot on the page, he glared at the book as if he'd like to rip it to shreds. "Horrid place to spend a couple decades."

Brushing his arms off with the palms of his hands, he let his gaze rove her body. "Well," he said, with one eyebrow cocked. "Hello there."

GREAT cheap fUN

Discover eBooks!

THE FASTEST WAY TO GET THE HOTTEST NAMES

Get your favorite authors on your favorite reader, long before they're out in print! Ebooks from Samhain go wherever you go, and work with whatever you carry—Palm, PDF, Mobi, and more.

SAMHAIN
PUbLISHING LTD

WWW.SAMHAINPUBLISHING.COM

Printed in the United States
122048LV00001B/154/P

9 781599 988122